PENGUIN BOOKS

1959

THE HAMMERSMITH MAGGOT

WILLIAM MOLE

WILLIAM MOLE

The Hammersmith Maggot

PENGUIN BOOKS

Penguin Books Ltd, Harmondsworth, Middlesex
AUSTRALIA: Penguin Books Pty Ltd, 762 Whitehorse Road,
Mitcham, Victoria

—

First published by Eyre & Spottiswoode 1955
Published in Penguin Books 1963

—

Copyright © William Mole, 1955

—

Made and printed in Great Britain
by Petty & Sons Ltd, Whitehall Printeries, Leeds
Set in Monotype Times

Ascribed in affection to
LADY NORAH

Chapter One

CASSON wondered why the banker was getting drunk.

It was not merely unusual and unpleasant: it was unique. Henry Lockyer never permitted himself to become intoxicated by anything, especially in his Club. Casson had often watched him in Cane's, watched him with the same fervent and amused curiosity with which he observed the grave antics and the tortuous follies of all his fellow human beings. Lockyer was a reserved man: dry and unemotional. He was impeccably neat in his dress, precise in his movements, punctilious in his routine. All this admirably fitted a Director of Gamman's Bank, which was one of the last, least known, and most highly regarded private banks in the City of London.

To Casson, however, this outward appearance fitted Lockyer too neatly. It fitted him so admirably that it might have been a staid fancy dress, an everyday disguise, behind which lurked dreams of piratical ventures and passionately contrived intrigues.

Regretfully – regretfully because he liked the savour of the unusual – Casson had come to the conclusion that the banker wore no disguise and that he did not dream. Henry Lockyer had a dull and earnest mind, one which mustered as high a degree of poetry as there was spite in the works of a grandfather clock.

It was because of this past disappointment in Lockyer that Casson now speculated. The dining-room of the Club was half-empty. Beneath the two massive chandeliers which lit the long room, in this severely pillared, gold-and-blue atmosphere, anguish was seething inside a stolid banker. Some private poison had been distilled by that unexciting brain, refined drop by drop in the methodical dusk which Lockyer carried in his head. Those irretrievable drops were spreading along his blood, infecting him, changing him into someone else than the Director of a Bank. Desperately the banker poured whisky on to his infection as one might pour oil on to a savage sea. At any moment Casson expected the storm to gain dominion and to see the leer of

7

Caliban break upon the ordinary features of the man who sat opposite.

'Evening, Mr Duker,' said George, the head waiter. Casson's full name was Alistair Casson Duker but all his friends and most of his many acquaintances called him Casson. Tradesmen's bills and Company Reports were addressed to him as Alistair C. Duker, Esq., M.C.; but when Marilyn Peploe had deluged him with letters insisting that he elope with her at once to Sardinia, she had merely and naturally and all-too-frequently addressed him as A. Casson.

'I will have smoked trout,' Casson said, glancing at the menu. 'Then the calf's liver à la française.' Cane's was famous among Clubs for its good food. 'Ask Daniel to step along, would you, George? I want a bottle of wine.'

Daniel, the wine steward, was the oldest of the Club servants, a short, grey-haired man with a head like an eagle and a prodigious memory. He loved wine and he loved Cane's: and that, Casson reckoned, was the sum total of his life.

'I'll have a bottle of Moselle, Daniel,' said Casson. 'The Eitelsbacher Marienholz '47.'

He returned to the pleasant itch of his curiosity about the banker. Lockyer always drank one glass of dry sherry before dinner and had two glasses of claret with his dinner, sometimes less, never more. This evening, in the small, oval antechamber to the dining-room where the members gathered for a drink before lunch or before dinner, Lockyer had drunk two double dry Martinis in fifteen minutes and was now starting upon his second personal decanter of whisky.

Casson leaned back in his chair, sipped his wine, and let his curiosity increase. This itch to explore had accompanied him through life, and he indulged it wherever possible. When just out of Stowe it had led him to become a dish-washer in a café on the Avenue Kléber in Paris, and as an undergraduate he had joined an ornithologist's expedition to find the nesting colonies of the flamingo in the swamps of the Guadalquivir. After the war, when he was demobilized from the Airborne Division, the itch had found a new excitement. He had been staying in Bath, relaxing from the mathematical fantasia of the battles for Normandy and

8

the Rhine, seeking the unaccustomed delights of grace in the Regency architecture of the Royal Crescent and the ancient luxury of the Roman baths. Rumour had come to him of an outbreak of mania in a village a few miles outside the city.

He had gone there for one night and had stayed a month. Those four weeks gave him a fascinating view of the margins of crime. He had begun to touch the sombre border region where desire, intensified by fear, becomes contemptuous of legality and where the sanctions of the spirit had shown themselves no deeper than medieval folklore.

To begin with, the inhabitants of the village had been coldly hostile to his presence. He had scrabbled irritably on the darkened window-panes of their suspicion. Gradually the shapes beneath the darkness had become visible and he had been able to reach down through layers of jealousy, hatred, and superstition. The yellow, stone church in the cup of the valley, possessed of a few fine memorials and indifferent stained glass, seemed a sure part of the villagers' weekly thought. But behind it Casson had detected the smoke of the Beltane Fires and the elusive menace of the Green Man who moved to a rule of his own in the heavy woods beyond the Openlea Farm.

He had uncovered a stew-pot of constricted rage and had saved an innocent woman from being driven demented. Above all he had been fascinated by the behaviour of human beings when they live in a world beyond the law. He had exorcized himself of this particular nightmare by embodying it, suitably disguised, as an article on the persistence of pagan theophany. His *The Witch of Bath* had been published in a London quarterly and had had its brief day of sensation. It had closed the case but it had not cured the itch. Casson searched for human oddities as another type of collector might seek after faked Rubens.

While he watched Lockyer, the itch told him that he had found another bizarre *objet d'art*.

Women drink because men drink or because they are in physical pain: sometimes because they have lost a lover, more usually because they have lost their looks. They never drink when they are happy. Men are more difficult, more double-faced. They drink for both reasons: to swell happiness or to dull misery. Lockyer

9

was not happy: that much was perfectly plain. But why was he miserable?

He was a bachelor. Had he at last proposed and been refused? Had he become unbearably lonely, as bachelors sometimes do? Or had he – a far more intriguing speculation – had he committed some crime against his business ethics? There was an extensive range of possible disaster open to a banker.

Lockyer had put down his knife and fork and, with his head in his hands, was leaning over the remains of his roast chicken, staring down at the mangled drumstick. Without lifting his head he called: 'Daniel! Come here. Bring me some more whisky. These damned decanters are no good. Bring me two more. Y're s'posed to be a wine steward, aren't you? Well, bring some wine . . .' His voice trailed off. Daniel took care not to catch Casson's eye as he fetched another of the small decanters. A party of four at the end of the room stopped talking for a moment.

With satisfaction Casson finished his liver *à la française*. It was excellent, a fitting accompaniment to the Moselle. He was doubly pleased since it was he who had found the new French chef for the Club, a risky experiment and one that had succeeded. He debated in his mind whether to go on to cheese, decided against it, paid his bill, and went out into the Oval Room, settling into an arm-chair with a glass of Armagnac. He was certain that Lockyer could not last much longer and he wanted desperately to be on hand at the moment of collapse.

He was swilling the brandy round in his glass when Daniel came through from the dining-room. Casson lifted a finger and the old man came over to him.

'You may know, Daniel, if Mr Lockyer has a room at the Club this evening?'

'No, sir. Oh, no, sir.'

'I think, Daniel, that Mr Lockyer and I will go home together. He has some port at his house which I wish to taste.' Daniel made a motion with his head, and his eyes never flickered. Casson went on: 'As a matter of fact I sold it to him some years ago – a Warre '27. I wish we had some of it here.'

'Yes, sir. Shall I ask Mr Lockyer to join you here, sir?'

'No, no, Daniel. He'll be along in a minute.'

'Yes, sir.'

But it was some time before Lockyer appeared. When he did he was unsteady. He stared round the Oval Room, swaying slightly, propping himself with one hand against the jamb of the doorway. He gazed at the portrait of Lord Palmerston over the fireplace, then transferred his gaze to Casson. There was apparently some recognition. He lurched over and dropped into an arm-chair beside him.

'Howyou, Casson m'boy?' he said. 'Have a whisky?'

Casson calculated. Lockyer was just drunk enough to be belligerent. Quiet men often were. Now was not the time to take him home. Another drink and he would be ready.

'Armagnac, thank you,' he said. 'Why not join me?'

'Rotten stuff,' Lockyer said in a loud voice. 'French stuff. Y'should only drink whisky. Daniel! bring me a whisky. 'Magnac here for m'friend.'

Lockyer leant back and seemed to relapse into a stupor. He jerked forward and muttered: 'Poking and prying. Can't leave a man alone. Filthy minds they've got.' With some difficulty he turned his head towards Casson. 'Ever been persecuted?' he asked, and without waiting for an answer, went on, 'You wouldn't be. You've got to be someone to be persecuted.'

He took his drink from Daniel's tray and set it down carefully on the floor. Then he pointed at Casson, who had been waiting for this moment.

'Lawyers'll tell you the greater the truth greater the libel. Isn't true, Duker. Isn't true at all. Greater the lie greater the libel. Nothing succeeds like a lie. Nothing at all. I've proved it. You believe me. I'm telling you something. A lie's worth money. Truth's worth nothing. You believe me. . . .'

He leaned back again in his chair, staring at the opposite wall, focusing. He closed one eye, then opened it quickly. It was clear that the remnants of self-control had not quite left him. The skeleton in Lockyer's cupboard had begun to dance, but as yet it remained behind the shut door. Casson waited patiently.

Lockyer sat forward and groped on the floor for his drink. He took a gulp of whisky and balanced the glass on the leather arm of the chair.

'Dirty little minds,' he said. 'Makes you sick. Like slugs. Know about slugs?' he asked.

'No,' Casson replied encouragingly.

'Crawl over things,' said Lockyer. 'Leave a trail. Sticky. Ugh!' He swayed and with some difficulty, very slowly, set down his glass on the floor.

'Must go home,' he muttered. 'Feeling a bit ill.'

He tried to get up but fell back into his chair.

Casson left him there and went down to the hall.

'Oh, Broom,' he said to the head porter, 'I'm going back home with Mr Lockyer. Can you find his address? I've forgotten it. He's – er – not too well.'

Broom found it in his card-index of members. Launceston Street, w8. Casson went back upstairs. Lockyer was sitting on the arm of his chair, unsteadily contemplating the carpet. Casson yawned.

'I'm going home,' he remarked. 'I'll give you a lift.' He hoped that Lockyer would neither know nor remember that he himself lived in a flat in Mount Street. If he did recollect he might suspect that Casson was not merely being charitable to a drunken fellow member: and that suspicion could make him close up like the silent figure he usually was.

Lockyer nodded and lurched towards the door of the Oval Room. At the head of the curving, double staircase down to the hall of the Club, Casson gave him a helping arm. Angrily Lockyer threw it off but almost fell down the stairs. He made no further motion of protest as Casson helped him down, collected his bowler hat and umbrella, and steered him out into St James's Street. Lockyer slumped into the front seat of the car, leaning back, breathing heavily.

He said nothing while Casson drove him home, and Casson did not wish to interrupt his silence. He luxuriated in the soundless power of the big maroon-and-black Rolls which was his joy and extravagance. His mind was also busy with the problem of how to unlatch Henry Lockyer's skeleton cupboard. The rattle of bones among the grotesque sentences of the banker's speech had raised his sense of curiosity to an insatiable pitch.

Launceston Street was deserted under the April lamplight and the squat, late Victorian houses had a mellow, contented look as if they were settling happily into yet another London Season.

Lockyer was able to walk without assistance to his own front door, though his feet were uncertain on the steps and he fumbled for the keyhole. Casson had followed him up the short patch and the four steps to the door, hoping that the other man would invite him in, hoping that he was not too sober to produce the ghost which haunted him, hoping equally that he was not suddenly seized by the implacable dignity of the very drunk.

Lockyer put his umbrella in its stand and laid his bowler carefully on a wall-table. Then he turned to Casson.

'Thank you,' he said. His speech was just detectably slurred and he swayed slightly. 'That was courteous. Come in and take a nightcap with me.'

He poured whisky for both of them, put the glasses on the dining-room table, pulled up a chair, and sat down. Casson followed suit. They must look, he thought, like some strange midnight Board meeting if anyone peered through the uncurtained window and saw them sitting solemnly at the bare mahogany dining-room table.

'I read *Witch of Bath*,' Lockyer said abruptly. 'Fellow in the Club told me you'd written it. I mus' tell you I thought it a lot of nonsense. Invented, you know.' He paused. Casson held his breath.

'I offer you apologies,' Lockyer went on. He made a motion as if to bow but quickly sat straight up again and gripped the table edge. 'I now believe it could be true. I will tell you why.' They always do tell, Casson thought in secret triumph. They must tell. They talk because the burden is too great to carry alone. In the end everybody tells someone of their hasty crimes or shameful errors. And then, when the ghost which lived in their brain is brought out and dangled before you like a pathetically menacing marionette, when it is made to do its grinning little dance on the polished table-top, it looks silly or sickening and fit only for the rubbish-bin.

''Fore I tell you,' said Lockyer, 'I must make it clear that I tell you in the strictest confidence.' Casson nodded faintly and the banker continued, 'Some days ago I was in the drawing-room after breakfast. I was reading the *Financial Times*. I always do. Except on Sundays, when I read the *Economist*. I remember that it was a warm morning. The window was open at the bottom. I state these details,' he added, staring fixedly at Casson, 'so that you may reconstruct the – er incident. Ten minutes before I was due to start for the City – ten minutes before ten, mus' be exact – my man Dobbie came in. Said there was a visitor. It was unusual, since I make it a rule never to interview people at my house. However, Dobbie gave me a message from this person. It was to the effect that he had come to see me in connexion with the Boys' Sailing Clubs. So I felt it my duty to see him.'

He paused. He seemed to be sobering up; but it was probably no more than a skin over a seething cauldron.

'You will not, of course, know what the Boys' Sailing Clubs are. I will explain. You may know that I am myself interested in yachting.' Casson did know. It was Lockyer's mania. 'I have recently conceived the project of setting up Boys' Clubs at yachting centres round the south and east coasts. Boys from the poorer districts of London, especially those in the earlier stages of juvenile delinquency, would be given holidays at these camps. They'd learn about sailing, the sea and, with good fortune, a few might decide to enter the Navy. It is not primarily a recruiting scheme for the Navy but – er – an attempt to give these boys some knowledge of what I might call the – er – manly virtues.' He leant both elbows on the table and pointed a finger at Casson, almost upsetting his whisky tumbler in the process.

'I have consulted many interested 'thorities on the matter – privately, of course. My scheme is in its final stage of planning. All that remains is to launch an appeal for money. I myself am giving the sites for the Clubs, but we shall need a considerable amount in order to build the clubhouses and to pay the instructors. My Committee has agreed to my suggestion that we should maintain secrecy until the appeal is launched. We hope thereby to achieve greater effect for our publicity.

'Consequently, very few people know of my scheme. Only the members of my Committee, my private secretary, and the technical consultants at the Bank.

'I was, therefore, a trifle surprised when this person – a Mr

Bagot he called himself though I am now inclined to think that that is not his name – wished to interview me on such a matter. I was afraid that he might be a person from the Press.

'I saw him – 'fact, I felt that I could not do otherwise – and he made a most improper suggestion to me.'

Casson raised his eyebrows.

'That is to say,' Lockyer hurried on, then hesitated, took a gulp of whisky, and brushed his hand vaguely across his face. 'We mus' be precise. That is to say he blackmailed me.'

Casson whistled softly and leaned forward.

'Blackmail?'

'It was most unpleasant.'

'You paid him?'

'Yes.'

Casson shook his head sadly.

'You shouldn't. You shouldn't. But they nearly always do.'

'It was an impossible situation,' Lockyer retorted with some vehemence. He finished his glass and refilled it. 'It's all very well for you to sit there and be wise. But this person Bagot exhibited what I can only describe as diabolical cunning.' Casson sighed to himself, wondering again at the astonishing *naïveté* of business men. 'He proposed to blackmail me for something I had not done.'

'But . . .'

Lockyer was not to be interrupted.

'He blackmailed me for being a homosexual.'

Casson stared at him. For the tick of a second he wondered if it were true.

'Observe his cleverness,' Lockyer explained, focusing his stare on Casson's tie and speaking slowly. 'I am a bachelor. I have a man-servant in the house because I do not like women. It is possible that you yourself are wondering whether this man Bagot was correct. Once the suspicion is in your mind, can it ever be eradicated? I suppose I had better assure you that I am not – that way,' he added bitterly. Casson shook his head.

'Of course not. But why on earth did you pay?'

'Bagot said that he wanted a thousand pounds. If I did not pay him at once he threatened to enter an action against me in

the Courts for accosting him in the Green Park and making inde-
cent suggestions to him. He showed an uncanny knowledge of
my movements. He named a day and a time when I had accosted
him. It was the day and the time when I had walked home through
the Green Park. I have no doubt that he himself was there.

'He pointed out that my interest in my Boys' Sailing Clubs
would only 'stantiate the accusation against me. Furthermore,
whether his suit succeeded or failed, I should have to resign from
the Committee of the Clubs, or the appeal for money would have
no chance of success. Indeed, such an action against me would
almost certainly ruin the whole scheme.

'He explained a good deal more. He seemed to have talked for
hours but I suppose it was only ten minutes because I arrived at
the Bank at my usual time. He explained that I was completely
powerless. If I handed him over to the police he would maintain
his accusation and no one would believe that I was being blackmailed for something which I hadn't done. I could not prove that
I had not done it. If I refused to pay, then he would bring his action
and, whether he won or lost, the smear of perversion would remain with me for ever. He himself would be safe because I could
not prove that he was blackmailing me.

'He said that, if I paid him and kept silent, I should never see
him again. . .'

'And you believed him?'

'Yes. He outlined to me his theory of crime. It was most convincing. He held the view that most criminals are discovered only
by repetition, by returning to the scene of their crime. He himself
would never blackmail the same person twice. Therefore, once I
had paid, I was safe. I paid.'

'Thereby sealing your presumed guilt?'

'Yes. He pointed out to me before I paid that I should be safe
from him in the future because he did not wish to be caught and
so would not visit the same victim twice. He on the other hand
would be safe from me because, by paying him his hush-money,
I had tacitly admitted the truth of what he accused me. It was, he
said, a double insurance policy which I, as a business man, should
appreciate.' Lockyer laughed shortly.

'We got a taxi. We drove to the Bank. I cashed a cheque for a thousand pounds. I went outside and handed it to him. He put it in a suitcase and vanished. I am a thousand pounds the poorer and I have given away my peace of mind.' He thumped the table and the tumblers rattled. He pushed the decanter towards Casson.

But Casson was drawing ovals with his finger-tips on the polished surface of the mahogany, ovals which interlocked in an interminable pattern.

'Do you want me to find him?' he asked, without looking up.

'No.'

'What's he look like?'

'No. I don't wish you to find him.'

Casson shrugged.

'He will blackmail other people. They will go through the same sort of purgatory. What about them?'

'Why do you think I've lost my peace of mind?' Lockyer retorted. 'Of course I've thought of them. But I've also thought of my boys. How many boys shall I save from the back streets? To how many of them shall I teach something finer than the ethics of the snack-bar and the coffee-shop? How many will find something else in life than cinemas and child-prostitutes and cheap silk shirts? And how many victims will Bagot blackmail? Which is the greater number? Which is the number I owe my duty to? Tell me that and I'll know what to do. But don't sit there comfortably and tell me to go to the police.' He was becoming quite heated, and Casson was pleased to find that the reserved, the punctual banker was capable of genuine human emotion, even of a sort of wayward poetry of passion.

'You mistake me,' he replied equably. 'I was not smug. I was thinking. Would you like me to catch this little man, this impish and careful Bagot – without involving you?'

Lockyer finished his whisky.

'You couldn't,' he said.

'What does he look like?'

'Neat, common, insignificant. I doubt if I could recognize him again. . . .'

'There must be something about him. . .'

'Nothing. He was a little taller than I am – about five foot ten.

He was probably forty – or fifty. He was thin and clean shaven and his teeth were normal. He wore a raincoat without a belt, a green hat, and brown shoes. He wore heavy, horn-rimmed spectacles and his hair was dark brown and parted in the middle – a habit which I personally dislike. He had a trace of accent. He was very clean – face, hands, nails.'

'Accent?'

'I can only describe it by saying that it sounded rather "common". You understand?'

Casson nodded.

'The only noticeable thing about him are his spectacles and his hair,' Casson mused. 'Therefore it is reasonable to assume that they were false.'

'Nonsense. I'd have noticed a wig.'

'Not a wig,' replied Casson, elaborating his own thoughts. 'Real but false. He had darkened his hair, parted it differently, put on the spectacles for the occasion, or put on different spectacles. Without them you might find it hard to recognize him, especially if he is so undistinguished. Have you ever seen him before?'

'No,' said Lockyer without hesitation. 'Definitely not.'

'But if you say that you wouldn't recognize him again, why shouldn't you have seen him in the past and not recognized him when he blackmailed you?'

'Possible, I suppose. I don't think so. Have some more whisky?'

Casson accepted, filling both their tumblers.

'How could he have learnt all that about you? About your Boys' Clubs in particular?'

'I don't know.' Henry Lockyer went on squirting soda-water into their glasses. 'Why bother to ask? I am sure that his name is not Bagot. You are sure that he does not look like my description of him. He is sure that he will not appear again. How can you catch him? He is a nobody, a common, unnoticeable little man. Thousands like him queue for buses day after day. . . .'

'No, they don't. He's different. He has a brain of a sort, courage of a sort, ambition or greed of a sort. And it is of a compelling sort or he would not turn to crime. He has a personality. No man can disguise his personality. He must betray something. Tell me the story again. Tell me every detail, however ridiculous, however trivial. Here's how!'

Automatically Lockyer drank some of his whisky in reply. Then he told the story again, word for word, minute by minute. He told it very well and in exact sequence. He told it without a ray of humour. Casson, trying to pierce behind the dry narrative to the personality of Bagot, was not bored. He even remarked to himself on Lockyer's unusual capacity for observing detail. One incident, in particular, intrigued him. The blackmailer had singled out for notice a marble bust in Lockyer's possession.

'There you are,' said the banker when he had finished. 'What does that tell you?'

'I don't know. What was his motive?'

Lockyer shrugged.

'Everybody wants money. Some have bills they can't meet, some have bills they want to run up. What else can you call his motive except money?'

'Within limits, I agree. The sort of bills they have to meet will tell you about their characters. Give me a man's receipts for a year, and his demand notes, and I'll tell you what he is like: within limits. You're a banker. You should know that. Read a man's pass-book and sum him up – even his dreams: but only within limits.'

Lockyer played with his glass.

'Yes,' he said. He sounded doubtful.

'What bill did he want to pay?' Casson went on. 'A mistress?'

'No. Oh, no,' said Lockyer quickly.

'Why?' Casson was alert. Something lay in that swift response. It was too definite.

Lockyer hesitated.

'He was a very common man,' he said. 'He would not have a mistress.'

'Common people are human,' Casson reminded him with a smile. 'Very human. Why are you so definite?'

Lockyer was silent for at least a minute. Then he said slowly and not without embarrassment:

'I'm sure he hadn't. You see, I don't like women. I – that's to say, they don't enter my life. I don't need them. I could feel that in him. I'm certain he wouldn't have a mistress.'

19

'A wife, then: who wanted a fur coat: who needed an operation: who nagged him to buy a house?'

'No. He isn't married. At any rate not now.'

'Again why?'

'I've always had a memory for detail. I noticed that one of the buttons of his raincoat – and he kept it buttoned up – continually slipped out of its buttonhole. Just as continually he fastened it again but it was an automatic gesture and I'm sure he was unconscious of it. It did that because the button was not properly sewn on, not as a woman would sew it. It was sewn too tight, too close to the material of the coat. I know because I've had to do it myself when I was a young man. If he had been married, his wife would have sewn it on for him and it wouldn't have slipped out. Also he had toothpaste on . . .'

'Toothpaste?'

'In the corner of his mouth. I imagine that his personal habits are meticulous and that he brushes his teeth after eating breakfast. He had left a trace in the corner of his lips. If he had said good-bye to his wife that morning she would have noticed it and told him to wipe it off.'

'She might have been in bed, or away visiting her children, or blind?' Casson suggested, letting his own imagination play. He badly wanted to pin Lockyer down on this point.

'She might indeed,' the other replied. 'But, in Bagot's obvious walk of life, the odds against each alternative are long. I am sure he is unmarried. I would go so far as to say' – he paused and an extra trace of colour seemed to suffuse his cheeks – 'that he was a – that he had never had a woman.'

'Go back to the bust.'

'The bust?'

'Yes. In your story. When he admired it.'

Lockyer rose to his feet.

'Come and look.' He led the way through folding doors into a back room. It was furnished like a woman's sitting-room, and its pale green walls were hung with French engravings. But a mahogany pedestal desk stood in front of the window and a large radiogram was massive in a corner. In the window embrasure, outlined against the drawn grey curtains, was a white marble head of a young man. It stood on a column of green marble. Lockyer pointed to it.

'That's the one. Roman. First century B.C.'

Casson contemplated it.

'It's a fine one,' Lockyer added.

'And little Mr Bagot admired it,' Casson mused, stroking his chin. 'He admired it greatly, so you say. He admired it so much, that common man with the mackintosh, that he took the trouble to remark upon it. He interrupted his blackmail to go and touch it, to admire it, to show his envy. He knew when it was carved – without your telling him. In the middle of his ten carefully planned minutes of crime he forgot himself so far as to comment on the head of a young Roman noble. Indeed he betrayed himself!'

'You know him?'

'Oh no. But I shall find him. I know what he is like. I know why he blackmailed you. I know how he can be found. That bust will send him to prison.'

Chapter Two

SLOWLY Casson drove the Rolls home to Mayfair. He could not be troubled to leave it in the garage, and parked it in the cul-de-sac which led into the gardens behind Farm Street Church. It was a warm night and it would come to no harm. He walked the eighty yards up Mount Street to No. 100a, let himself in, and took the lift up to his flat on the third floor.

He put down his gloves on the table in the hall and switched on the lights in the broad library beyond which looked south across the gardens. A vase of white lilac came up suddenly and startlingly out of the darkness and flaunted its Spring fervour against the bookshelves which lined the room.

He went over to the windows, drew back the curtains, and leaned out. The gardens were locked and deserted, alive only with the faint river-sound of a night breeze. He stared at them, seeing, not the black and jet green of the trees, but a dozen shadow shapes of the man Bagot, all of them faceless, each of them elusive. What was the little man like? What was his ambition? That, in particular, he desired to know. Find a criminal's ambition and you find the criminal. You find also another mind to explore, a mind that is exciting in its own curious way since it is prepared to go out beyond the law, prepared to be hunted, in order that it may satisfy its craving.

He turned back into the room and lit a cigarette, wandering round, chasing the thought inside his head, running his finger-nail along a line of book-titles to try to catch some clarifying association from them, some random word that would link together the details which he already knew. Somehow Bagot must become real. He must become mentally coherent in that room so that he could be visualized and thus known.

Casson went into the scullery and took a bottle from the cellar. He poured himself a glass of Yquem, pulled an upright chair over to the library window and sat there, twirling the glass between his fingers, making a living man from Lockyer's marginal comments on Bagot's single, colourless, and undoubtedly disguised appearance.

He had a trace of accent – 'common' Lockyer had called it. He was neatly, almost primly, dressed – so far as could be seen despite his mackintosh. He would be lower middle class. The odds on that were a near certainty.

He was not a manual worker. His hands were smooth and neatly kept. Lockyer had particularly remarked on that fact. Therefore he would be an office worker, a clerk of some sort, earning perhaps nine pounds a week. No. That theory would not fit.

Bagot had showed an uncanny knowledge of Lockyer's affairs, of his personality, of his movements. He must have studied his victim closely, have watched him, followed him, observed his ménage in Launceston Street. In that case he could not be a clerk, bound to rigid office hours. He must have the free time in which to study his quarry. He must be, to some extent, his own master; a small tradesman perhaps. Unless – and this was a grotesque thought – he was a clerk who devoted his annual fortnight's holiday to a single *coup* of blackmail! It was an amusing thought but not a practical one. Blackmail was a profession, not a hobby.

Casson stubbed out his cigarette and leaned back in his chair. He was pleased. The blurred picture of Bagot was being brought into focus. The unobtrusive little man with the tight raincoat button was being caged in thought.

Casson was inclined to agree with Lockyer's view of the button. Bagot was unmarried. He lived alone and looked after himself. It was indeed an eminently rational supposition since a wife would be dangerous to him in his illegal profession. She might be extravagant with the money which he lifted from his victims. She might buy herself a fur coat, take an expensive holiday, insist on having a servant: thus draw attention to her inexplicable source of income. Or she might be afraid of his activities, afraid of her man going to prison which, in the street where she lived, would mean social desertion and sidelong, sneering looks from her neighbours when she went to the shops. He would be scared of her too, in case she confessed his secret to her closest friend, who would undoubtedly tell the whole street. No – Bagot must be unmarried.

Nor was he a womanizer, a suburban Casanova. He was no

timidly frenzied lover of some exorbitant chippy who blackmailed him with the withdrawal of her flaunted body – her only dazzling possession – so that he blackmailed others for the money to re-conquer her affections. Lockyer had been positive on that point; and Casson was prepared to accept his view since the banker himself was frightened of women. Like calls to like and, in this respect at least, Lockyer and Bagot recognized each other.

Casson took a gulp of Yquem and 'chewed' it before swallowing, a taster's trick, savouring to the full the deep, scented body of the golden wine. His mind swerved lovingly to the Sauterne vineyards, then returned to Bagot.

He hesitated before he pursued his line of reasoning. He lingered, with a connoisseur's pleasure, on the verge of his next thought, desiring to savour it in anticipation. It was the keystone of the arch in which he was framing the figure of the blackmailer. It was the Roman bust.

This was the oddity in Lockyer's story and Casson believed it to be the most significant fact of all. It was unusual for small tradesmen to show such an involuntary and passionate interest in Roman sculpture: doubly unusual to show knowledge of the marble art in the century before the birth of Christ. You cannot conceal your personality, however hard you try, and this love of, or avarice for, works of art was in Bagot's nature.

Casson puzzled until he was too tired to think. He went to bed, read a chapter of *Mansfield Park*, and fell asleep, his mind soothed by the delicate and slow-paced intelligence of Miss Austen's miniature world.

The next morning he walked leisurely down Berkeley Square, along Bruton Street and Bond Street to his office. The traffic in Vigo Street compelled him to halt and, while he waited to cross, he contemplated with satisfaction the outward aspect of his firm. Two Georgian windows framed the front door, over which was written in unobtrusive gold letters *Manton, Heywood, and Partner, Merchants in Wine and Liqueurs*. It looked more like a private house than the offices of a well-known firm of wine merchants and Casson had been at pains to preserve its atmosphere of quiet courtesy and fine living. The sale of good wine was not merely a trade by which men lived; it was also one of the niceties of civilization and should, therefore, be conducted in a graceful manner. Furthermore, the atmosphere was one of the firm's assets: many of Casson's friends liked to drop in after midday and broach a bottle of Manzanilla with him. Friendship grew into custom and both parties were content.

Tippett, the head clerk, in his frock-coat, was standing behind the counter when Casson entered.

'Good morning, sir.'

'Good morning, Mr Tippett,' Casson replied, passing through into his own office. He always addressed Tippett as 'Mr'.

Casson settled down to his letters and a perusal of the 'abstract' book. At eleven he called in Tippett.

'We will taste, Mr Tippett.'

'Yes, sir.' A spasm of enjoyment passed across Tippett's iron-grey countenance. From the mahogany glass-rack on the wall he took two tasting glasses and wiped them carefully with a duster until they glittered icily in the morning light. He uncorked six of the small, eighth-size, sample bottles which stood on the side-board. While he watched the preparations Casson smoked a cigarette. He never tasted without one. When reproached by his friends he would cite the example of one of the finest palates in the Douro, the owner of a Quinta, who never tasted port without a cigar.

The two men examined, compared, and adjudicated upon the growths of Burgundy which had been submitted to them for laying down. When they had finished and Tippett had gone back to his counter, Casson stood by the window, idly contemplating the people who passed by outside. He was counting his good fortune. He was thirty-seven, almost thirty-eight, but still a young man. He was fit, interested, and sufficiently well-off. He was a bachelor and his own master; his own master too in business since he had inherited the firm from his champagne-minded Victorian father, extending both its list and its custom. He appreciated beautiful things. He turned to glance with pleasure at the wall over the fire-place where there hung a landscape by Théodore Rousseau.

The keystone fell into place. The Roman bust settled perfectly into the mental arch. Bagot was his own master. He was a man without family, without relationships. He desired beautiful things.

The theory was grotesque but not impractical. Casson believed it to be true. Bagot blackmailed to satisfy his ambition. His ambition was to create for himself an ivory tower, a life apart from the harsh bustle of the world, a small universe in which he was the lonely monarch of looted beauty.

Casson took his gloves and went out. If Bagot had blackmailed once, he might have blackmailed before. If he were not known by name, or by previous conviction, he might be known by his activities: and the repetition of crime always led in the end to the discovery of the criminal. Go to the police! Their multiple memory was as long and omniscient as records could make it.

He walked briskly up Savile Row to the West End Central Police Station. It stood squat and functional in white concrete, looking up New Burlington Street with the same stolid efficiency as that of a policeman on his beat.

Casson waited while the uniformed constable in the entrance hall took his name and rang through to the C.I.D. He was shown upstairs and into a plain office. It was furnished with a desk, a swivel chair, a hatstand, a leather arm-chair, and an untidy bookcase in which there was, of course, a frayed copy of Stone's *Justices Manual*. The walls were bare except for an etching of the Grand Union Canal near Maida Avenue in the Paddington Division in which Strutt had begun his police career.

Superintendent Strutt, George Barnard Strutt of 'C' Division, sat behind the desk, pushing a paper-clip round the surface of his blotting-pad with the chewed end of a pencil. He glanced up as Casson entered the room, then bent back to his game.

He was a man of forty-two and, for a policeman, unusually shaped, being short and fat – paunchy was the coarse description – and piggy-eyed.

'Well?' he grunted. Casson sat down.

'I need your help.'

'Naturally.'

Casson sighed to himself. Strutt was in a temper and when that happened he took time to placate – time and lager. In the end he always helped. He liked Casson.

'I am hunting a blackmailer,' said Casson in as melodramatic a tone as he could muster. Strutt reached for a writing pad.

'What's his name?' His voice was uninterested.

'Bagot.' Strutt made no motion to write. Casson settled himself into the uncomfortable arm-chair. 'As you will already have guessed, my brilliant and beautiful bogey,' Casson continued, 'Bagot is not his real name. It is, as we say in the underworld, an alias, a *nom de guerre*, a clean handle. How clever criminals are!'

'Yes,' said Strutt. 'I've read about them in books.' Casson relaxed. Strutt was coming along nicely.

'I have his description,' Casson continued. 'In fact, I have two descriptions: the one he uses for blackmail and the one he uses when he goes to bed at night and gets up in the morning. The latter is a deduction. Beyond that we know nothing: except what I have invented ...'

'... that will be plenty.'

'But it will be the truth. Now before I unfold to you this unpleasant little story, I must warn you that it's off the record. The victim does not want Bagot found and will not give evidence against him if he is found. But I wish to find him because I dislike such people. He has a cold, mean mind and he will blackmail some other frightened innocent.'

'And, of course, you like the man-hunt?' Strutt suggested with a twinkle in his small eyes.

'You could put it that way,' Casson agreed. He told Strutt the whole story, including Lockyer's name. He had no compunction in doing this since he knew that the banker was safe and that every detail might help. When he had finished giving Lockyer's description of Bagot, he added:

'Now, as you will agree, that particular appearance is one which he uses only for blackmail. His ordinary appearance will be different. But it will not be very different. He would know that his disguise must be as normal as possible so that the victim believes it to be real and gives it, if he gives it at all, to the police as the real and undoubted description. Therefore it will only be a slight change of the blackmailer's ordinary appearance.

'So what does he do to disguise himself? He makes his hair darker, not by dye but by hair oil. He parts it in the middle – a thing which the victim would automatically notice. He wears heavy spectacles. Undo these things and you have the real Bagot,

27

a man of about forty-five, with mousy hair parted on the side, and wearing light-rimmed spectacles. He will be neat in his habits, has clean, unspoilt hands, and is five foot ten in height. Find that one if you can.'

'Easy,' Strutt replied equably. 'There are seven thousand of them in the West End every day.' He threw his paper-clip into the metal waste-paper basket. 'What do you want me to do?'

'Listen.' Casson told him the rest, displayed before him the personality which his mind had created of Bagot, described the place of the bust in the arch of mental invention which framed the blackmailer. Strutt stared at him while he told the tale. At the end he shut his eyes.

'I think you're wrong. I think you're being too clever about this art business. I think he's a pervert.'

'Why?'

'Why should he think up this accusation of homosexuality? Because it's in his mind. He's probably keeping some boy in a villa in Harrow. Sex and money. That's how crime works. Wicked.'

He reached for the telephone.

'Yard, please. Criminal Record Office.' He gave them the two descriptions of Bagot and Casson's imaginary character-study, leaving out the incident of the bust and merely saying that the wanted man might be interested in antiques. He put the receiver down.

'I'll let you know,' he said.

'Come in on your way home and have a drink at my flat,' Casson suggested. 'I hate being seen in public with people who only drink lager, and I've come by an early Colette novel which you can borrow – one of the ones she wrote under another name. It'll amuse you.'

'Right, boy,' said Strutt, grinning. His hobby was French literature. 'Six sharp. Mount Street. We'll have hanged your man by then.'

Chapter Three

CASSON strolled down to Cane's for lunch. In the oval ante-room he met Nigel Willington, and the sight of the gaunt, cadaverous figure gave a practical twist to his ideas.

He ordered a sherry and went over to Willington. As they stood there together, they illustrated unconsciously the witticism which an ornithologically-enthused member had minted about the pair of them: remarking that Willington resembled a vulture bending patiently over the merlin Casson in order to snatch a scrap of the latter's kill. Willington, indeed, looked like a young vulture. Though only thirty-six he was prematurely grizzled. His great height gave him a stoop and his heavily wrinkled features the appearance of a sad man of fifty. But Nigel was quite unlike his appearance, being a cheerful soul, a permanent optimist who found nothing wrong in the world. He had two children whom he was delighted to spoil. He was Managing Director of Willington and Company, Antique Dealers, of Sackville Street, London, and he loved his job, having a flair for fakes and a ruthless joy in discovering and rejecting them. His wife, Sally Honor, regarded him with respectful amusement and their house in Stafford Terrace, w8, was an untidy and friendly shambles.

'Do you sell much Roman stuff?' Casson asked him. 'Busts and so on? First century B.C. or A.D.?'

'No. People don't have the space for them. Busts are a bore. You can only put 'em on a pedestal and the char knocks 'em off. Why?'

'I've become interested in that period.' Nigel gazed at him with a sad eye.

'You treacherous fellow,' he remarked. 'You lie to me.' He sighed. 'Men were deceivers ever. You are no more interested in those centuries than you are in the geological formation of Cheshire. You are, I suppose, chasing some harassed malefactor?'

Casson agreed readily and added: 'I'd be grateful if you'd

get one of your assistants to check any catalogues you've got of forthcoming sales and see if there is anything – busts or figures – likely to be of an early date: and then let me know. Do you keep any record of who bought what at past sales which your men attended?'

'Sometimes. If it's an article that interests us. We might make an offer later on.'

'Could you let me know the name of anyone who has bought such stuff – not merely busts – during the past two years? The purchase must be fairly small: not too big to go into a typical "parlour".'

'It will take a day or two,' said Nigel. 'We're jammed up with our scheme for this year's Antique Dealers' Fair. But I'll send you the catalogues and get a man to check on the back sales as fast as possible. Is it a murder?'

'Lord no,' Casson replied with a grin. 'I'd never get a look in at a murder. The police are far too good.'

'Pity,' murmured Nigel. He finished his gin.

'Come and lunch?' Casson suggested.

'No,' Nigel replied, peering at an old, enamelled, French watch which he took from his coat pocket. 'I'm lunching at the Savage. Someone wants to sell me their collection of snuff-boxes. One's got a portrait of Lady Caroline Lamb on it. Rather fun. I'll ring you later this week.'

Casson lunched alone and went back to his office. He wrote to a shipper, ordering twenty dozen Burgundy, finished some personal correspondence, and strolled home. Intrigued though he was with the quest for Bagot, he deliberately prevented himself thinking of it since he felt that Strutt was about to disappoint him. When he arrived at six that evening the Superintendent would probably hand him a full record of the real Bagot, would know precisely who he was and exactly where to find him. Then the chase for the shy and dangerous animal would be nothing more than the setting of a trap for a marked fox.

Strutt arrived late, sweating from his walk in the warm evening. He mopped his face, ran his finger round the inside of his collar, and plumped down on the sofa. Without a word Casson handed him a tall glass of the iced lager which was his favourite drink.

Strutt drank most of it in one breath, put down the glass, and snorted.

'Hopeless,' he grunted. 'Ruddy hopeless.'

Casson was mixing himself a dry Martini and did not look up.

'Defeat,' he mused, 'is such a stimulating experience. It encourages action.'

Strutt had pulled from his pocket a creased envelope which he held straight before him, studying the shorthand notes on the back.

'Both your descriptions were impossible,' he said. 'As you knew they would be. The age and the height didn't help. You'd be surprised how many criminals there are who are five foot ten and about forty-five. None of them is a blackmailer. So the boys tried your line about curiosities. . . .'

'Curiosities?'

'Yes. You know. Curly rubbish.'

'Antiques?' Strutt nodded impatiently and continued:

'They were interested in that one. But they drew a blank.'

'So our friend Bagot remains a shadow, a whisper of fear, a nightmare with an accent.'

'I'd call him a louse.'

'And where do we go from there?' Casson inquired with a trace of malice.

'Hemel Hempstead,' said Strutt. Casson smiled at him. Strutt loved keeping a trump card up his shiny blue sleeve.

'Delightful. Why?'

Strutt merely pointed at his empty glass. Casson refilled it, placing the jug within reach of the Superintendent. Strutt took a deep draught.

'Two years ago,' he said, 'a fellow called Greenhaugh committed suicide. Drove his car into a canal up Hemel Hempstead way. A Humber it was. They had the hell of a job getting it out. . . .'

'Was he alone?'

'Yes. You don't take a chauffeur if you're going to croak yourself.'

'Then how did you know he committed suicide? The steering might have gone? Or he fell asleep?'

31

'A bloke in the brick-works nearby saw the car. It was during the dinner break. It stopped, waited for about ten minutes. The man inside threw away a cigarette. It started again, heading for the canal, engine roaring. It went straight through a fence, straight into the canal, and Bob's your ruddy uncle. I spoke to one of the boys who was on the case and he said Greenhaugh came out looking just like a drowned rat. It seems he had sharpish features.' Strutt sniffed. Casson never quite knew whether the policeman's comments resulted from a macabre sense of humour or a memory trained to record each detail.

'He was the junior partner of a small export firm in Mayfair,' Strutt continued. 'Been going ten years and quite prosperous and had not reached saturation point. Greenhaugh could have made more than he was already making. He had quite a decent income – better than mine,' Strutt added. 'A wife and three nippers in Dunstable, no debts, no vices, no reason to croak himself. He was a Freemason, a Rotarian, and a Methodist. That is to say, he had been the last two but he was giving them up because he thought that they might make him *déclassé*. Shows how stupid he was. His wife told us all this and it seems she took it with great seriousness.'

'A snob.'

'Keen as mustard. She was a cousin of a daughter of a Peer or something like that and wanted to move back into that world. Anyway she couldn't help and we couldn't find anything.

'Fortunately his bank statement arrived the day after he had done himself. His wife let us see it. The last entry was the day before. It was for six hundred pounds paid to "Self". Quite a tidy sum to draw in one go.

'I went along to the bank, a branch of Lloyd's in Mayfair. The Manager wouldn't tell me much anyway. The Bank Act, very proper, you know.' Strutt snorted, drank some more lager, and wiped his neck.

'All the cashier could say was that Greenhaugh had come into the bank at half past ten, said he wanted six hundred pounds in one-pound notes for an urgent business deal, collected the money, and gone out. The cashier thought it a bit odd, especially as Greenhaugh looked rather flustered. But Greenhaugh said his partner wasn't there to countersign a cheque on the firm's account and the Manager agreed his own account could stand it so that was that. I'd like to see mine agreeing that I could cash one for six hundred quid.'

'So should I,' said Casson.

'We checked with his firm in Charles Street. They knew nothing of any business deal. There was no money in his desk. None in his safe. He had an appointment for lunch that day in the Mayfair Hotel. He hadn't cancelled it. All his secretary could tell us was that a man had called to see him, had stayed in his room for quarter of an hour, and they had gone out together. The visitor carried a brown paper shopping bag such as you buy for sixpence at Harrod's, gave his name as Martin, and was so ordinary as to be hard to describe.

'It looked like blackmail. But how? His wife knew nothing. I didn't expect she would. I got her to lend me all his files of personal accounts and I spent a week-end going through them. He was one of those meticulous and untidy blokes. He kept everything but without method. By the time I had finished sorting his papers, I could have kicked him into the canal myself.'

Casson chuckled.

'I worked out his income and his expenditure,' Strutt went on. 'They tallied exactly and every year he saved a bit and bought a few shares. I found out that he was saving to buy a small farm on the estate of his wife's remote and titled relative – hoping, I suppose, that they'd get into the snob swim that way. The only thing I didn't understand was the size of his personal expense account. It was between five hundred and fifty and six hundred and fifty a year. Twelve quid a week. Quite a lot; especially as he also had an expense account with his firm.'

'So you looked for his mistress?'

'Who's telling this story, blast you? There wasn't one. Not a trace. I went through his papers at the office. Then I found her. Six years back in a bank statement. Henrietta Kavenagh Martin. I found two cheques, fifteen guineas each, one seven days after the other, paid into a bank at Hatfield. Then a regular monthly payment of five quid a week. Or rather twenty quid a month on a Banker's Order. I understood the size of his expense account.'

'You say her name was Martin?' Casson queried, leaning forward. Strutt took no notice.

'She was a black girl – West Indian. God knows where he had picked her up. Cardiff, probably. He had business down there. I reckoned the two payments of fifteen guineas were for a hospital or a doctor, and we traced her that way. She's a nice kid and she sews like an angel. Matter of fact I got her to make a blouse for Adeline's birthday last year and Adeline thought it was first class. . . .' Casson smiled to himself. He could picture George Strutt giving it to his pretty blue-eyed wife with whom he was still as much in love as when they married twenty years before.

'This Martin girl had a child by a white man – not Greenhaugh. Or so she told me. Quite a decent nipper but you know what half-castes are, poor devils. It isn't right, you know. She was Green-haugh's mistress. I suppose he found her a change from his wife. Anyway Greenhaugh had come to see the girl about an hour before he died. She said he was almost incoherent and kept asking her if she had been followed around by a strange man. Matter of fact she had been. In the end the strange bloke had picked her up in a teashop but she'd given him the brush-off. When he heard that, Greenhaugh – as she picturesquely put it – swore an oath, said he'd look after her as well as he could, gave the nipper five and twopence in loose change, and beat it. The girl was a bit worried but she had strict instructions never to communicate with him. An hour later he drove into the canal.'

'What did the man look like?'

'Greenhaugh?' Strutt asked casually.

Casson finished his drink.

'The chap who followed the Martin girl.'

'His description would fit that of the Martin who called on Greenhaugh at his office. He wore heavy spectacles. He wore a brown suit. He wore a raincoat: and a green hat.'

'Or it would fit Bagot?'

'Or it would fit Bagot.'

'Isn't it strange that both the blackmailer and the girl should be called Martin?'

'Isn't it! If it was blackmail.'

They looked at each other in silence. The lager jug was empty. Casson rose to refill it. When he came back he said:

'And that's all?'

'That's all.'

'But why did you pick the Greenhaugh case out of the records?'

'The boys have always reckoned it to be a blackmail case. I had them pick out all the unsolved ones. This seemed to fit.'

Casson smoked half a cigarette while Strutt scowled into the empty fireplace.

'Why six hundred pounds?' Casson asked.

'Why not?'

'And Greenhaugh's own credit was sufficient to meet it?' Casson persisted.

'Yes. It overdrew him a bit because he'd had a lot of bills the month before. But his credit would stretch that far: just that far.'

'So Bagot got into Greenhaugh's office by using the name Martin, by suggesting somehow that he came from the girl in Hatfield,' Casson whispered, trying to picture the scene. 'He blackmailed him with the threat of the black child who wasn't his. He took him down to his Bank – the same technique as with Lockyer. He probably told him that he wouldn't blackmail twice. Greenhaugh, being a wary business man, wouldn't believe him. He thinks there will be another touch. If he pays again, bang goes the rest of his savings. So he drives slap into a canal, hoping, I suppose, that it will be considered an accident. But it isn't. And he wouldn't have been blackmailed twice. So it's all a waste anyway. And, if he'd lived, he'd have been such a worthy snob.'

Strutt levered himself to his feet and tucked his shirt down into the strained waist-band of his trousers.

'Anyway,' he chuckled, 'I got the name of a damn good seamstress out of it.'

'You callous fellow,' Casson began, mocking him, but got no further. Strutt half-closed his small fat eyes and tapped Casson on the chest.

'Listen,' he said grimly. 'I don't give a damn for Greenhaugh and I care even less for Lockyer. I want to get the crawling runt who soaked them. I don't like him. He turns my stomach. He makes me queasy. He sours my beer. See?'

35

'I see. Shall I find him for you?'

Strutt sighed. 'I wish you would. I can't. I haven't the men. I've got too many other cases in hand. And even if I did find him I couldn't prosecute him. One of his victims is dead and the other won't give evidence.'

'You could give him a tough time?' Casson suggested.

Strutt grinned. 'Yes. We'd make it hot for him. All right, boy. You find him and I'll turn the heat on when you've found him. Now, where's that book you promised me?'

Casson picked it off the table by the lilac. It was an early novel by Colette, *Claudine à l'école*, published in 1900 under the name of her first husband 'Willy'. Casson had had it bound in green and speckled leather. He thoroughly enjoyed acting as pander to Strutt's passion for French novels and the French tongue, admiring the obstinacy and devotion which had made him and his wife go to night school to learn the language and which had cajoled them, every possible year until their son – Casson's godchild – was born, to spend a blissful ten days bicycling in Touraine and Normandy.

Strutt took the book and looked at it greedily. Then he slipped it inside the folds of the evening paper which he had brought, reached for his hat, shook Casson's hand, and was gone. Casson laughed gently and with real affection. He mixed another Martini and walked over to the window to watch Strutt on his way to catch a tube at Hyde Park Corner. In a moment the bulging, squat figure of the policeman moved through the gardens, its head glancing backwards and up for a second in salutation towards the windows of Casson's flat.

Then Casson frowned. If he discovered Bagot, or Martin, or whatever he was called, Strutt would take over. Strutt wouldn't let him finish the case himself: indeed he couldn't do so because of the evidence needed later in Court. How could he contrive to remain in at the death?

He shrugged, and went into his bedroom to dress for the theatre. That problem could wait. It was going to be hard enough to find Bagot. The only possible line of inquiry was the black-mailer's interest in Roman art; and on that one incident in Lock-yer's study, on the few words which Bagot had uttered about the bust, on his unusual knowledge and the gleam in his eye which

Lockyer had described when Bagot fingered the carving, Casson had erected a structure of personality which might be completely false.

He went out to see the Lunts in *Quadrille* and, in the extreme sophistication of their acting, forgot the ordinary-looking little man who drove people to suicide and despair.

The serpentine speculation returned to him later when he was sitting at dinner in the Savoy Grill and his host's young Italian wife was entertaining him with a baroque account of the latest disappointments and indiscretions of Roman Society. She was a strikingly handsome girl and, while she talked at him, her eyes were never still. They were looking at his face and hands, her gaze travelling up and along the outline of his fingers and the arc of eyebrow and ear, as though she were storing up each separate anatomical curve so as to string them together when he was no longer with her. He was aware of this devouring and disintegrating gaze. He was equally aware that it was, in its frank sensuality, almost entirely unconscious.

But, even while he felt her stare measuring him, his mind was busy with the little man whose real name was neither Martin nor Bagot. What was he doing at that moment when he, Casson Duker, was eating Sole Waleskwa? Was he sitting, alone and silent, in a Finsbury attic, absorbed by an intricate meditation which oscillated between a Worcester vase and the financial status of his next victim?

The Roman girl beside him was whispering to him how much she admired the English sense of discipline – an admiration, Casson felt, which was founded upon an adamantine determination never to follow the same code – when the two words clicked and another element fell into place in the creation of Bagot's imagined personality. Roman. Discipline.

Bagot admired the severity of the Romans, the Puritanical harshness of the Republic, the humourless restraint which they imposed upon their emotions. Bagot was at heart a Puritan, humourless, precise, reserved, fanatical. The execution of his *coups* showed the careful practicality of his planning. He never asked too much. He never stayed too long. He never let greed overcome strategy. He would admire Roman Generals. Perhaps

37

that was what had brought him to admire Roman art. Or vice versa. And he too would be dominated by his ambition: not in his case to build a State of Wealth but to erect a private imperium of beauty.

Casson hoped again that his imagination was not playing him false. The world was mostly imaginative and it would be a deprivation if this dream proved not to be true.

The next morning there arrived at his office in Vigo Street, sent by hand from Nigel Willington's own office round the corner, a large, flat envelope full of catalogues of approaching auctions. Rapidly Casson skimmed through them, searching for any offer of Roman antiquities. But there was little; mostly it was Georgian silver, pictures, and a fine set of William IV chairs which was to be offered at Sotheby's.

During that week he was so busy dealing with the rush of orders in preparation for the height of the London season, champagne for débutante dances: hocks, Burgundies, and Cognacs for regimental dinners: clarets and more champagne for Ascot week: that the enigma of Bagot lay like a curled snail in a corner of his mind. It stirred once to irritate him when Nigel sent along a list of those who had bought antiques of the right period from his own firm during the last year. The list had been marginally annotated by Nigel himself. Two reproduction Roman urns . . . '*bought by a Scottish nobleman – God knows why*'; a marble statue of Hercules capturing the Nemean lion . . . '*bought by a museum: it was once painted red by Lord B—s on his twenty-first birthday.*' And three more items.

Casson threw it into a bottom drawer of his desk. It was quite useless.

In the next few days and during the week-end, which he spent in Suffolk, he became more and more irritated. He hated being beaten.

On Monday morning he drove straight to Willington's. When he got there he found Nigel standing in the middle of the showroom, contemplating with a vacant stare a magnificent cabinet.

'I'm sure its a copy,' he remarked. 'They say it's Louis Quinze.' He leaned forward and touched it. 'A fellow in Paris used to copy them. Beautifully done.'

38

'I want you to buy me a bust,' said Casson.

'Oh, yes. Of whom?'

'Anyone. First-century Roman. Preferably a man. A woman might do but not a girl.'

'For the malefactor?' Nigel queried, his fingertip searching along the sides of the cabinet. Casson nodded, forgetting Nigel was not looking at him. 'Why not a girl?' Willington asked.

'The malefactor is a man. He doesn't like girls.'

'But a woman?'

'He might not mind. Roman matron stuff. Strong, severe, and pure. Besides, it might appeal to his mother complex, if he has one. Preferably find me the head of a young man.'

'It'll cost you a bit.'

'I won't lose.'

'What'll you do with it?'

'Sell it. I want you to sell it for me. At Christie's. With enough publicity.'

Nigel frowned at the cabinet.

'Why?'

'To attract a criminal.'

'It's nice to know when one's barmy,' Nigel observed mildly. 'I suppose you do, eh?'

'Not in the slightest. I'm entirely logical. The only thing I can lose is a gamble on a guess. It wouldn't be the first time.'

'No. Nor me. I'm not going to buy this piece. I guess it's a copy. But I'll get you your bust. Come and dine next Saturday. We've got a cook, and Sally would love to see you.'

In the course of the week, windily and abruptly a return to winter with the chestnut blossom flung wastefully on the pavements and in the gutters, Casson received his novel back from Strutt. Inside the parcel was a note which said with some economy of space:

Dear Casson, thanks very much. We both enjoyed it. Adeline sends her regards. Sincerely, G.S. P.S. Have you found him yet?

Casson grinned as he tore up the note. Strutt delighted to needle him.

Nigel produced a bust for Casson's inspection when he dined

39

in Stafford Terrace that Saturday. Casson walked round and round it with approval while Sally, whom Casson had known from her childhood, made rude remarks on the haircut, morals, and obvious temperament of the original model.

'Is it genuine?' Casson asked.

'I think so,' Nigel replied. 'At least Heskett says so and he should know. I haven't the faintest idea.'

'Beautiful bait,' Casson murmured, moving round the white, marble head to catch it from different angles. The blank eyes, its close curled hair, and its handsomely, unintelligent features appeared serenely oblivious of his curious delight. 'Beauty in wait,' Casson went on, still circling the head like a hunting animal stalking its prey. 'Beauty as a trap. A marble orchid to catch a fly. No man-trap ever looked like this. Ho!'

Sally stirred uneasily.

'Don't be horrible, Cass,' she protested. 'You gloat.'

'I do,' he said. 'I gloat, my dearest Sal, because I am going to catch with this beauty a man who might one day blackmail your daughter.'

'Oh,' she said, and changed colour, and went downstairs to the kitchen to see that the children were not annoying the cook.

Casson could not bear to leave the statue with Nigel over the week-end. He took it back to his flat and set it up on the table where the lilac had been. He was vastly pleased. That type of trap appealed to some tortuous compartment in his mind.

His housekeeper, Mrs Baker, who arrived on Monday morning to make his breakfast, was swiftly unenthusiastic. She referred to it as 'a nasty, white thing that caught the dust'. She refused to believe in his plot, the basic element of which he told her. This had become a habit of his since the day when, purely out of curiosity to see what her reactions would be, he had given the rosy-faced widow a copy of *The Witch of Bath*. Her comments had proved direct, pungent, and wise.

Willington's had arranged for the bust to be auctioned by Christie's in three weeks' time. Casson waited patiently while the first three weeks of May went by and then, as the day of the auction approached, the excitement of the gamble took hold of him again.

He went down to Spencer House early on the Friday of the auction, securing for himself a perch on the window-seat by the auctioneer's desk, from which point of vantage he could see the faces of the buyers. The long, tall room filled steadily, and by the time the auctioneer mounted his rostrum there were people standing two deep round the walls. Nigel squeezed in beside him on the window-seat.

The sale was mostly of pictures: two Zoffanys and a Hoppner: a School of Tintoretto: a sporting picture by Marshall for which the bidding was especially keen; and, as usual, thought Casson, a Guardi. God knows how many pictures Guardi must have painted.

He spent the time selecting faces from the intent crowd, faces and ages to suit Bagot – if he were there. He found seven which might fit and drew a rough seating plan of the room on the back of his programme, marking in with crosses the seven possible people. He scribbled on the top of the programme: 'Do you know any of these?' and passed it to Nigel.

Nigel completed his comments and handed the programme back. He had identified three of the men as dealers or dealers' agents. A fourth was a known collector and, added Nigel in his medieval-looking script, even better known at Crockford's as a fine bridge-player.

Casson was reasonably sure that none of these could be his man. He felt instinctively that Bagot was not a dealer. He turned over a page and wrote: 'Has any of them an accent?' The reply was swift: 'Yes. The collector. He is a Pole.' That left three men.

The auctioneer came to the bust. It was placed on a high table for all to see. Casson gave it the merest glance.

The bidding opened slowly: heavy pauses between the raises; a sticky response, dull, uninterested.

An intervention sent the bidding up. It spurted for twenty pounds, then languished. But Casson had time to catch the flick of the programme from the new bidder and his heart sank.

Bagot had not come to his lure. Instead it was a woman, well-dressed in black, a diamond clip in the lapel of her coat, a small, expensive hat perched above the determined face.

The bidding slowed again.

'Do you want your bust?' Nigel asked.

'Yes,' Casson whispered back. 'I do.'

'It may be expensive?'

'Yes.' If Bagot would not take it, he himself would.

Nigel flickered his programme. The bidding rose ten pounds. The woman followed the price up. Then she stopped. The hammer fell. The bust, still blankly staring at the rows of people, went to Willington's.

Nigel chuckled, scribbled on his programme, and slid it on to Casson's knee.

'You owe me ninety quid. Why not go fishing? It's cheaper,' he had written.

'The pike might recognize me,' Casson returned.

'Pike calling to pike . . .' Casson saw Nigel scribble, when his eye was caught by a movement near the door.

One of his selected suspects was leaving. But he was accompanied by a woman. Definitely not Bagot. That left two. Disappointed, angry because his beautiful snare had failed, he surveyed the remaining two. Then he went rigid.

Two bronze statuettes were up on the table: a boy with bow; a boy with javelin. Seventeenth century. One of the possible Bagots was bidding.

He must be in his late forties, an ordinary man with mouse-coloured hair and a cheap brown suit. He wore gold-rimmed spectacles. His gaze was fixed on the auctioneer.

The bidding went up in fives and his programme flickered to keep it rising. Casson stared at him, fascinated, instinctively certain, excited.

'Ever seen him?' he whispered to Nigel.

'No.'

The bidding rose. Casson clenched his hands, praying that one of the big dealers would not send the price over the mousy man's ceiling. At last the bidding slowed and stopped. The last gesture had been from the flickered programme. Casson gazed and waited.

'Sold!' announced the auctioneer. He pointed to the man in the brown suit and asked his name. The man muttered something which Casson could not hear, wrote on a slip of paper and passed it up to the clerk. The auctioneer went on to a set of silver spoons.

Casson ringed the two crosses on his programme which showed the positions in the room of the only two men who could still be Bagot. He showed the programme to Nigel and said: 'Come along.'

Together they moved round the outside of the room, edging their slow way between the chairs and the people standing against the walls. When they reached the opposite side of the room, Casson stopped and contemplated Suspect No. 6.

The grossness of his features became apparent. But he was still eligible. Lockyer's description had been vague enough for Casson to fit it to seven people in that one room. Then the man lifted his left hand and scratched his scalp: and Casson knew he was not Bagot. His index finger was heavily stained with nicotine. Lockyer had been precise on the subject of Bagot's cleanliness.

That left No. 7. Only No. 7. Casson drew on his programme a heavy arrow pointing to the cross which marked No. 7's position, handed the card to Nigel and whispered:

'Watch him. Hear him speak if you can . . .' 'Do you want his name?' Nigel interrupted. 'I can probably get it for you.'

'No. If he is Bagot, the name will be false. If he isn't Bagot, it doesn't matter. But come out when he leaves and tell me. I'll be in the car. In St James's Place.'

He slipped out of the auction room, went downstairs and sat in the Rolls, waiting.

It was over half an hour before they appeared. The inconspicuous little man came first, carrying a parcel in brown paper. He looked round, then walked towards St James's Street.

Nigel strolled over to the Rolls, lighting his pipe.

'He paid for it in pound notes,' he remarked to Casson. 'Wanted to take it away at once.'

'Did you hear his voice?'

'Yes.'

'Was it "common"?'

'A trace of accent.'

Casson started the engine and drove towards St. James's. At the end of the street a slim figure in a brown suit, a figure who was standing awkwardly because he was balancing a brown parcel on his hip, was signalling for a taxi.

Chapter Four

BY the time the Rolls had reached St James's Street, a taxi had jammed itself across the traffic and stopped by the kerb. Bagot – it *must* be the blackmailer since everything fitted so exactly the picture of him which Lockyer had described and which Casson had created – Bagot was bent half-way into the taxi, presumably laying his parcel on the seat, only his rump showing.

Casson memorized the number of the cab and slid the Rolls into the traffic, drawing ahead. The cab pulled out from the kerb and followed him into Arlington Street. From its station by the traffic lights he judged that it would turn left by the Ritz into Piccadilly and would go on westwards. He kept ahead of it down the long sweep of Piccadilly to Hyde Park Corner and, watching it in his driving-mirror as they rounded the Artillery Memorial, guessed that it would enter the Park.

At Albert Gate it passed him, and he let it go away up the Carriage Road by the Barracks, easily keeping it in sight but screened from it himself by two intervening cars. In this fashion it led him down Kensington Gore and along Kensington High Street. To Campden Hill? No. It crossed the Campden Hill Road junction, still going west. At Hammersmith Broadway it was stopped by the traffic policeman and Casson let the Rolls hang farther back in the line of cars, sure of the cab's next direction. When the traffic moved again, it led off and, cramped by a chara-banc, he lost it. He let the Rolls out in a burst of speed and caught it, keeping closer. Surely its only possible destinations were Hammersmith, Chiswick, or Kew; or at the farthest Brentford? The nearer it was to its destination, the less he could afford to let it out of his immediate sight. A sharp turn when he was blocked and it was invisible, and he would have lost it. The vital moment would have come and gone, thrown away, unused, only remotely and by luck to be conjured up again.

In King Street, Hammersmith, shortly after the Town Hall, it turned left. Casson hesitated. He knew that the streets which led down left to Chiswick Mall were residential, comparatively empty of traffic. The black-and-maroon Rolls would be conspicuous and, if Bagot had noticed it in the Park, its second appearance might lead him to suspect. Nevertheless Casson followed. He could do nothing else.

As he turned up the street, he reached into the dashboard cupboard for tinted driving spectacles and a tweed cap which he always kept there. He slipped these on, feeling foolishly theatrical.

It was just as well. The taxi was drawn up half-way down the long street. Apart from that, there was no other car. Casson accelerated.

The street was like one of those in a nightmare: interminable, empty, staring. Although the Rolls swept up it at speed, it seemed only to crawl along the vacant length. But it passed the taxi as a flash. Casson was able to catch the number of the house before that one into which Bagot was stumbling, his brown-paper burden clutched in his arms. In the same moment he glimpsed a slur of paleness as Bagot's face was turned to the Rolls. But he could only have seen the back of Casson's head and then the car was away, safe, slowing down to turn into Chiswick Mall.

As he braked hard, Casson glanced at the white plaque which carried the street's name. Bickersteth Street, w6. The house-numbers on Bagot's side of the street were unevens. The number Casson had glimpsed was 49. The house nearest to the Mall was 87. Therefore Bagot's was 51. Mr Blackmailer Bagot of 51 Bickersteth Street, London w6. Got him!

Casson drove fast back to Mayfair, elated. He confessed to himself ruefully that he was also relieved. He had by no means been certain that the gamble of the bust would pay off. Indeed, he still had to prove that he was not the dupe of a convincing coincidence.

He parked the car in Savile Row, went into Manton, Heywood and told Tippett, who was changing his frock-coat and preparing to go out for lunch, to bring him in some smoked salmon sandwiches. He went himself down to the cellar and chose a bottle of Louis Roederer '45, feeling this to be the most suitable form of libation to the baroque gods of gambling.

While he waited for Tippett to return he pored over a large-scale street map of London, learning by heart that area which included Bickersteth Street. When he had finished the sandwiches, he filled himself another glass of champagne and leant back in his chair to review his strategy.

First he must prove that the man who lived in Bickersteth Street was Bagot. Intuitively he himself was certain. But intuition was not proof and there was only one man who could make suspicion into fact. That man was Lockyer. Therefore, somehow, he must show Bagot of Bickersteth Street to Henry Lockyer. And he must show him, not as he had seen him that morning at Christie's in his ordinary, everyday garb, but in his disguise as a blackmailer, with the heavy spectacles, the hair falsely parted, the misbuttoned raincoat. Therefore he must catch Bagot when Bagot was 'on the pounce'. But how to bring him and Lockyer together at that crucial moment: unseen to each other: one frightened to identify, the other terrified of detection.

It added up to this. He must stalk Bagot, stalk him night and day, watch him as a hunter in his hide watches the tiger circling round the tethered goat. Then, the proof being reached, Bagot could be given to Strutt as a gift, a gift which he himself could insist on helping to wrap for its delivery to the Public Prosecutor.

In his flat that evening he got out a battered suitcase and washed from its surface the pre-war luggage labels which said Seville, Toledo, Madrid, Narbonne. Beneath pyjamas he packed three worn shirts without the maker's label, a razor-case and hairbrushes, also without initials, a Leica camera, a pair of binoculars, and two albums of photographs. He had taken them of buildings in Bath and Brighton and Edinburgh in preparation for a book which he had once planned to write on Regency Living, and they would now serve him as his disguise.

Next morning he took the Tube to Stamford Brook, walking from there across King Street and down British Grove to Chiswick Mall. When he reached the Mall he put his suitcase down and leaned on the railing, looking at the river. It was a bright, fickle May morning with an undecided breeze. Small, puffed clouds littered the blue sky and the light on the water was not a steady summer glow but brittle sheets of silver green. It was low

46

tide and two barges were leaning heavily on the bare mud, looking like torpid louts still unrecovered from the night's full swell of intoxication.

He picked up his bag and strolled on happily, sinking himself into the identity which he would assume for the hunting of Bagot. The Georgian façades of the houses along the Mall confirmed his intention. He would pose as an author writing a book on Post-Regency London. He would be interested in antiques. He would be, in his minor way, a connoisseur. Though not of sculpture. That was Bagot's province, and Bagot should be made to take delight in teaching him the aesthetic value of his looted treasures. If he were Bagot. Any other thought on such a morning was dull and not to be entertained.

He turned back towards Hammersmith and walked up Bickersteth Street. It stretched away northwards and, even in the playful May sunlight, it looked bleak: solidly, bourgeoisly bleak. It was lined by similar and respectable mid-Victorian houses, each wedged between its neighbours as if they stood shoulder to shoulder for support against free-thinkers, radicals, evolutionists, and Maypole dancing. Viewed through the eyes of a dabbler in Victoriana it was not an ugly street. It had the strength of its own convictions. It aimed at no pretence, it attempted no false Palladian grandeur which might have given it the troubled air of a grocer claiming an Earldom. It was a street made for small, mildly prosperous tradesmen and for their bustling, constricted family circles. In linear perspective it was faintly Canaletto, a deceptively infinite repetition of a single geometrical pattern. But it was cramped by the want of conception in its builder's mind. It lacked joyousness. It was a treeless avenue of moderate ambition.

Casson walked on steadily and came to the road which cut across Bickersteth Street. The corner house on the left-hand side was Bagot's. It showed no sign of life. He examined the houses opposite, on the right-hand side. It was in one of those that he needed a room. A lair that should be his hunter's hide. But none of them looked like a boarding-house and there was no 'Room To Let' notices on their windows.

He walked on, depressed. If he could not get a room opposite No. 51, a major part of his scheme would fail. He resolved to try

47

the local newsagent's shop. It might easily have advertisements of lodgings and, with luck, there would be one such house in his chosen area.

He was disappointed again. There were advertisements but they were all for lodgings on the north side of King Street or for furnished flats by Ravenscourt Park and Turnham Green. Nothing in Bickersteth Street. His inquiry of the man behind the counter drew an equal blank.

Casson went back down Bickersteth Street. He could not bear to leave it. And it was fortunate that he did so, for, as he passed No. 50 – the house on the corner of the intersection opposite to Bagot's – a middle-aged woman came out. Her dark hair, raven black, was gathered severely into a bun on the nape of her neck. Over her hair she wore a shapeless grey hat. She carried two shopping bags.

Casson seized his opportunity. He asked her if she could let him a room for a week or two. He exerted all his charm and, as he did so, he noticed that she must have been handsome when she was young, with black hair above a pale ivory skin. Only her brown, muted eyes must have modified that beauty and now, perhaps because the startling contrast of colouring was gone, they bore a baffled and disappointed look.

He explained that he was an author: that he was seeking a peaceful place in which to begin his book on Victorian London, a book in which would figure Bickersteth Street and its surroundings. At this glib recital in a voice which Casson knew by long experience how to modulate and manage to the fullness of its scale, her suspicion began to vanish. Grudgingly she admitted that her next-door neighbour, Mrs Gunn of No. 48, had a room free as her boy had gone off to do his National Service. Mrs Gunn might be able to accommodate him. Then she passed on her way down the street, her body stiff and preoccupied with the need for decency and the continuance of tiredness. Casson shook his head bitterly, condemning the incessant labour which so soon and so completely ruined the delighting gift of a woman's beauty.

Mrs Gunn was quite different. She had never been beautiful. She had never even been pretty. But she radiated good humour. Jolliness was the apt word. Without question Mr Gunn was a lucky man. Without question he ate well and did not suffer from nagging.

Mrs Gunn would give him a room for a fortnight. Yes indeed. She had met a writing gentleman during her annual holiday at Deal and he was a very lively gentleman. He had a fund of anecdote which Mr Gunn had thought to be, on occasion, a bit racy. She herself liked writing gentlemen. And fancy writing a real book about Hammersmith! It's an interesting place, the world, to be sure.

She showed him to the vacant room, a cosy room tucked up at the top of the house, surprisingly gay with patterned chintz and over-populated by a reproduction on the wall of Frith's *Paddington Station*. Her son, she explained, had gone to join what she called the Anti-Airforce, but she would look after her lodger just as she would her boy. All writing gentlemen liked to be undisturbed, so Mr Gunn had once informed her, and she would bring up his meals on a tray and of course he must give her a copy of his book when it was finished.

Casson looked round the room with pleasure. It was far better than he could have expected. It was clean and cheerful and it faced the right way. It would have been enervating to keep vigil from some rank and ill-furnished lodging. Furthermore Mrs Gunn was obviously attentive to the stomach.

He unpacked his few belongings, careful to shut back the binoculars in his suitcase. Then he went out to buy the tools of a writing gentleman's trade: a large packet of paper, a bottle of ink, and an ashtray.

On his way he thought to telephone Tippett, saying that he would not be in for three days. He calculated it would take him that time at least in which to establish some regularity in Bagot's movements; and not until then could he safely leave Bickersteth Street for a few hours and go up to Manton, Heywood.

Back in his room at No. 48, he got out his binoculars, pulled a chair up to the window, and began to study Bagot's house. No. 51 was obliquely opposite. Each window had net curtains and the top of each was two inches open, doubtless to air the rooms. Between a low brick wall along the pavement and the front wall of the house was a tiny square of garden. Others along the street, each the same size, were bright with pansies, a few tulips, or purple aubretia, but Bagot's was a grey square of crazy paving bordered by a privet hedge.

Casson studied the angles of light. He would have to be careful if he wanted to get a clear photograph of Bagot. He would need a telephoto lens and a lens hood. Even then it would be a chancy matter. He explored the neat bathroom across the landing and found that it would do admirably as a dark room, the curtains luckily still being lined with their wartime black-out material.

He lunched from Mrs Gunn's flowered-painted tray off meat-pie, apple-tart and custard. With some difficulty he managed to separate the custard from the apple and secrete it at the side of his plate under a piece of pie-crust. She talked to him the whole time and carefully he refrained from pumping her about the people in the street. Instead he showed her the albums of photographs which he had taken in Bath and Brighton, sure that she would carry the news of her gifted gentleman down the length of the street and thus build up his assumed identity. Furthermore, she would not comment if she happened to come into his room and see a camera set up there and pointing out of the window. Architecture would cover a multitude of investigations.

Throughout the afternoon he kept his vigil. Nothing happened. Not until six. Then Bagot appeared, shut and mortice-locked the front door behind him, and set off down the street towards the Mall. He was dressed as Casson had seen him at Christie's the day before. Casson noted the time and waited.

Exactly forty minutes later Bagot returned and let himself into the house. In the still street Casson heard the click of the latch and the heavier click as the door was bolted. He let half an hour elapse and went out himself, walking in the same direction which Bagot had taken. He hoped to find some place to which Bagot was likely to have gone.

He found three pubs within easy walking distance. Bagot might have gone to any of these. Or he might equally well have taken a stroll along the Mall. Casson hoped that it was a pub. That would make introduction easier.

When darkness had come down he took his suitcase and went to Mount Street. He left a note for his housekeeper, saying that he would be away for some days, and packed a camera tripod, a tele-photo lens, a lens hood, and some developing material.

The next morning he was up, shaved and dressed, by eight o'clock, and Mrs Gunn, when she came in at nine, commented with pleased surprise on his early habits. Writing gentlemen, she thought, never left their beds before eleven. He replied that his only eccentricity was that he preferred not to have his room done before lunch-time, trusting that this would give him at least four hours' solitude in which to take photographs. As soon as she had gone he set up the Leica on its tripod, fixed on the telephoto lens, and sighted it. It would as yet be too early to need a hood. That could wait until the sun was up. By the time he had completed these arrangements his poached egg was cold and he had to get rid of it in the bathroom. He left his tray on the landing.

It was worth a lost breakfast. Bagot came out of his house pre-cisely at nine thirty. He stood for a moment looking up at the sky. Casson managed to get two photographs before he moved off down the street towards Hammersmith. Casson did not bother to follow him, wishing to plot Bagot's daily routine before showing himself. He took several more photographs of the street opposite as a test for light and focus.

At a quarter to eleven Bagot returned. From his shopping bag projected some lettuces, a bottle of milk, a loaf of bread, and a roll of newspapers. Other, but invisible, purchases bulged in the bottom of the shiny, black bag.

He was not seen again for the rest of the day: not until early evening, when he left his house at six o'clock, punctual once more. This time, as on the previous evening, he walked towards the Mall.

Casson gave him a few minutes. Then went out himself. He felt that he must find the pub in which Bagot drank: if, indeed, he did go to a pub and did not merely stroll up and down the Mall, watching the traffic on the river.

Bagot was not in the nearest, the Larkrise. Nor was he in the Duke of Northumberland farther down. Therefore it must be the Shepley Arms. A glance at his wrist-watch told Casson that he had only five minutes to go before Bagot was due to leave and return home – that is, if he followed a definite routine – and on that hope Casson was gambling for the future.

51

Bagot was in the Shepley Arms. As Casson entered he was sitting in a corner, his tankard to his lips, just finishing a pint. He wiped his mouth fastidiously with a white silk handkerchief tucked into his shirt cuff – a detail which Casson put away in his mind – got to his feet and left, giving an incurious glance at Casson as he did so. For the first time Casson saw his eyes, and he was disappointed. They had nothing in them of what he had expected : no cunning, no animation, neither fanaticism nor malice. They were ordinary, slow, opaque eyes.

Casson ordered himself a pint of bitter. From now on if he were to scrape acquaintance with Bagot and drink with him, it must be beer. He sighed and drank it slowly, observing the barman, who was, so he gathered from the conversation, named Peter. Peter seemed a garrulous sort of man.

He leaned over the bar.

'Do you know that chap who's just gone out?' he asked. 'I'm sure I've met him but I can't remember his name.'

The barman looked at him.

'What chap?'

'The man who was sitting over there in the corner. He went out just now, just as I came in.'

'Oh, him. Yes. One of our regulars. Very quiet customer Mr Perry is. Regular in 'is 'abits. Orders a pint o' mild, drinks it, and goes off. Never 'as anythink else.'

'Perry?' he queried slowly, as if racking his memory. 'Umm. What's his Christian name?'

The barman started cleaning his teeth with a matchstick, a habit which Casson found distasteful.

'Blessed if I know,' he confessed. 'Doesn't speak to anyone much. Very quiet customer.' Then his face lit up and he took the match out of his mouth. 'Jock,' he said. 'That's it. Jock Perry. 'E's a member of our Christmas Fund. The Guv'nor got 'im into it.' He rummaged in a long flat drawer at the back of the bar. ''Ere you are,' he said. 'Perry – 2/6. I'm wrong. It's not Jock. It's John. Me memory must be going.'

'Oh yes,' said Casson, non-committally. But the barman was not to be put off.

'You live in these parts, sir?' he inquired.

'No,' Casson replied. 'I'm a writer. I'm doing a book about this part of London.'

'A writer, eh, sir?' He started rubbing his ear, regarding Casson doubtfully. 'Well, sir,' he added, 'if you want to know all about the neighbourhood you want to be in 'ere on Friday evening. Old George Stevens comes in and if you give 'im a pint and a chaser 'e'll tell you everything that's 'appened 'ere for the last seventy years. Regular old soak he is. I don't believe 'alf his stories. But it'll be all right for you, sir.'

'Why?' Casson asked in curiosity.

'Newspapers, sir. 'Ere today and gone tomorrow. Juicy little story tonight and a murder tomorrow, and the day after they're both flat as old beer.'

'I'm not a journalist,' said Casson, amused and treasuring up the comment to retail to some of his Fleet Street friends. 'I write books. The one I'm doing now is about the architecture of this area: photographs and all. Very expensive, I expect.'

Peter's expression changed.

'Ah, I see, sir. Beg your pardon.' He eyed Casson with a new respect, and Casson felt that he had found an ever-ready tap of gossip which he could turn on when he pleased.

'Have a drink?' he suggested.

'Thank you, sir,' said Peter briskly. glancing round to see if the Guv'nor was near, 'I'll 'ave a nice stout, thanking you.'

Casson chatted for a few minutes, nodded good night, and left.

John Perry! Otherwise known as Bagot. Otherwise known as Martin. John Perry, blackmailer, with two successful *coups* and one suicide to his credit. If he was the right man. If he was Bagot: or Martin.

Casson did full justice to Mrs Gunn's supper although he wished that she would make a savoury instead of apple tart and he missed his customary bottle of wine. Mr Gunn, he gathered, was safely ensconced in the kitchen, from which he only budged to go to bed.

'Comes in from work, he does, sir; puts on his slippers that I warm for him and settles down to his paper. Doesn't speak a word till he goes to bed. Says I talk enough for two, sir.' She chuckled happily. 'Regular caution he is.' Through the open kitchen door Casson had caught a glimpse, as he went up to his room, of wispy grey hair round a bald patch and a pair of pince-nez. So much for Mr Gunn.

Casson developed the film which he had taken that morning. When he had finished his patient labour in the warm darkness of the little bathroom he took the strip of negative into his bedroom, drew the curtains to, and examined the film against the electric light. The pictures were not bad. Whether they would enlarge to studio size he could not tell. If they did not they were almost use-less, the image on them being too small for easy identification. He hung the film up to dry, switched off the light, drew back the curtains, and gazed at the house of John Perry.

It was now dusk and there was a soft, flickering glow of light from Perry's windows. Casson could see little, for the curtains were closed, but when the idle breeze shifted them he could see the glow and could see it flaring on the indistinct outlines of the room behind. It was too fragile and yellow for firelight. It must be candles. But what was Perry doing with candles in that drab, dull house? Was he a miser? Was he sitting there, contemplating by the soft light his latest acquisition, the two bronze boys armed with their bow and javelin? Was he merely a quiet bachelor spending a legacy on the gradual collection of a few long-coveted treasures, building up for his old age a sparse and private museum?

The latter thought, and the probability of its being true, depressed Casson. He wanted to believe in his Bagot theory because it was outrageous and grotesque and he had found people to be both these things. But in this case, and in Bickersteth Street, the odds were against the grotesque.

He went to bed in a mood of frustration, tried to read a book about Syon House, tried to sleep, tried to read again, and finally fell into a drowsy coma from which he was awakened by Mrs Gunn with his breakfast.

'Poached egg, sir,' she said. 'As you liked it yesterday. Not pappy, sir. Can't abide any food that's pappy. Nice and firm.'

Casson inspected the egg. It was not pappy. On the contrary, it was superb. He felt better. He envied Mr Gunn. He set up the Leica and waited.

At nine-thirty Perry appeared. 'Regular in 'is 'abits.' He locked the door behind him and started down the path, raising his arm to put on his hat. Then he paused, and Casson got a photograph, full face. He turned back, tried the front door to make sure it was shut, and started off again, stiffly holding his shopping bag. Casson got another picture as he turned into the street.

Quickly he unloaded the spool in the darkened bathroom, sealing it into a numbered canister. He left the house, walked up to King Street, and took a taxi to Mayfair. There he delivered the developed negative of the first film and the freshly taken second spool to a photographic studio with instructions that the film was to be developed in Metol-Borax two bath developer so as to get maximum shadow detail. The prints were to be blown up to whole plate size if they would bear that degree of enlargement.

He took the taxi back to Bickersteth Street and was safely ensconced in his chintz-covered watch-tower when Perry returned to his house, his shopping bag bulging again with milk and newspapers and bread.

The front door closed behind the mild, spare figure of Perry and the street was empty, uninspiringly deserted in the sunlight. Casson settled down to wait, wondering for how long this daily routine would continue, wearily conscious of the high probability that the morning shopping and the evening half hour in the Shepley Arms were the basic pattern of Perry's outdoor life while the real and vital pattern was woven inside No. 51 Bickersteth Street.

But the outdoor pattern altered that same morning.

Chapter Five

CASSON had just sat down to write his story of the Bagot case from the night of his meeting with the drunk Lockyer up to his own first pint in the Shepley Arms when the door of No. 51 reopened and Perry emerged. Casson, taken by surprise, dived for the camera but he was too late. Perry was out of range.

In his excitement Casson put his hat on his head while still in his bedroom. He stood there, looking at his wrist-watch, giving Perry a minute and a quarter to get most of the way down the street. Then he slipped downstairs, let himself out, and followed.

To Casson, the pattern had altered drastically. Never had he heard of Bagot or Martin being clothed in anything but the same nondescript brown suit that Perry habitually wore. Now he was in a black City coat and striped trousers. He carried a neatly rolled umbrella and wore a bowler. He looked like a clerk on his way to the office in Moorgate. But why at half past eleven in the morning?

Casson followed him to Ravenscourt Park Station and, choosing the carriage behind him, boarded an eastbound train. As they rattled through Hammersmith and Barons Court, Casson's excitement became renewed depression. Perry might be going to his lawyer's, or to some respectable office from which he had retired and to which he returned two days a week in order to keep himself busy. Indeed, the only two things against him, the only two threads which linked him to the shadowy Bagot and the still more remote Martin of Hatfield, were his personal appearance and his purchase of antiques.

They changed trains at South Kensington. Perry walked primly down to the Circle platform and stood motionless and black in the strong daylight. He took the eastbound Circle train. Casson followed him. They got out at the Mansion House. Without looking round, Perry walked past the Bank and up Threadneedle Street. Opposite the National Provincial Bank he stopped and consulted his watch. Then he went on. Suddenly he turned into a door on his left and was lost.

Casson did not quicken his pace. He had marked the doorway and kept his eye on it while he covered the fifty yards to Perry's bolthole. He walked past it, glancing inside. He could see plates of cold lobster and dressed crab, neat piles of sandwiches under glass cloches, bottles of beer in buckets of ice. The snack bar was about half full.

He walked on, stopped, turned back, and turned into the bar – 'John's Bar'. As he entered, Perry had his back to the doorway, and Casson went to the counter on his right. Above the shelves on the wall of the bar was a mirror overprinted in gilt with the name of a sherry shipper. It was hanging at an angle, tilted forward, and in it Casson could see Perry across the room.

Perry was chewing a sandwich, a glass of beer on the counter before him. He was talking to a tall, fair-haired young man who was eating veal and ham pie. The young man also wore a black and striped City suiting.

Casson ordered a chicken sandwich and a glass of non-vintage champagne. While he ate he watched. The bar was filling up and the air was becoming pearly from cigarette smoke. Casson felt safe from detection, especially since there was no mirror over the counter above Perry in which he could have had a reverse view of Casson watching him.

The young man was tall, well built, and had that very fair hair which seems so fine in texture that it looks dead. He had a pleasant, humourless face and seemed to be no companion for a possible blackmailer. But, from his experiences in Bath, Casson distrusted appearances. During his investigations of the 'Witch' one of the nicest of the old women in the village had displayed a startling aptitude for intricate cruelty.

After half an hour the young man looked at his watch, finished his Guinness, and he and Perry left the bar. They walked down Threadneedle Street to the Bank, shook hands, and parted, Perry turning towards the Underground station and the young man continuing westwards.

Without hesitation Casson followed the young man. He might

be losing Perry at the critical moment but he wished to trace to its tip every tentacle of Perry's outdoor life.

In Poultry the young man turned into a large building. As Casson strolled on past it he saw with a spasm of surprise that in discreet bronze letters it was labelled, *Gamman's Bank*.

Ecco! And Lockyer was a director of Gamman's. The coincidences mounted into the region of inevitability.

Casson gave the young man ten minutes, during which time he could have washed his hands and returned to his post in the bank. Then he went in, walked up the long hall, and asked a question about currency exchange. While he was waiting for the reply he looked along the counter. At the far end, obviously in the junior position, was the fair hair and pleasant face. Casson waited. The answer came back: 996 francs to the pound sterling, 1,680 lire. Casson thanked the teller and strolled out, glancing as he went at the silver-and-black name-plate before the young man's place. Mr Macfarlane, it stated. The fair head never looked at him as he passed through the tall swing-doors.

From a call-box Casson telephoned Strutt. The fat Superintendent sounded irritable.

'Have you got him?' he said.

'Oh, no,' Casson replied. 'I'm just amusing myself.'

'Well, I'm not,' snapped back the voice. 'And I will tell you why, Dr Watson. Kent is playing Middlesex tomorrow afternoon and I was going to watch. Now I'm not. And I'm ruddy well not because some blasted burglar called Soap-fingers or Twinkle-toes or some idiot name has ruddy well pinched a mink coat from some idiot actress and I've got to find the oaf. See?'

'In this weather,' Casson observed, 'a burglar in a fur coat will look obvious. You should find it easy to catch him. Do you know anything about a Mr John Perry of 51 Bickersteth Street, w6?'

Strutt's voice altered.

'Is that Bagot?'

'I don't think so,' Casson replied evenly. 'But it may be a clue.'

'Clue!' snorted the Superintendent. 'Clue! You sound like the gutter Press. Why don't you find me a decent fingerprint and then bring me the finger that made it? All right. I'll ring you back.'

'I'd rather you sent a note to my flat,' said Casson. He had no desire to let Strutt know where he was spending his days. If Strutt knew that, he would horn in on the game too soon.

'All right. All right. What about two tickets for the first Test?'

'Certainly not,' said Casson, who could get them easily. 'You should be spending your time guarding honest citizens.' He rang off.

He took a taxi back to Chiswick, hoping to get there before the earliest moment at which Perry could have reached home. He paid off the cab at the end of Bickersteth Street, walked quickly back to his lodgings, and took up position in the window.

Seven minutes later Perry appeared, walking sedately down the street, his umbrella hooked over his arm. Casson, looking at his watch, made a calculation. Perry had returned from the City in just five minutes over the time which he had taken to get there that morning. Therefore he would almost certainly not have made another call on the way: so that Casson had lost nothing by following Macfarlane.

At six o'clock Perry went down to the Shepley Arms. Casson took the opportunity to go out and ring up his flat. Mrs Baker answered. He told her to open any note that had been delivered by hand that day and read it to him. Only one had come and it was from Strutt. It said:

Nothing known. No good. No tickets. Blast. G.S.

Casson went down to the pub. Perry was still there, two-thirds of the way through his pint. Peter the barman seized on Casson at once and introduced him to old George Stevens. Casson thought it best to play out his role of a visiting author, stood the old man a pint of mild and a double whisky chaser, and sat down with him in the corner opposite Perry. Let Perry get used to his presence!

The old man was interminably muddled. He forgot both the climaxes to his stories and the names of the celebrities in them. It was a tedious evening, but worth it if it helped to catch Perry.

Casson escaped as soon as he could and went back to Mrs Gunn's supper. Then he turned out the lights in his room and sat by the window until one in the morning, keeping watch. With exasperation he wished that Perry would leave open the curtains so that he could see what antiques – if any – littered the room behind. Or were the bronze statuettes his only possession?

The next morning Perry did his usual shopping and, in this period of grace when he knew where the little man was and when he would return, Casson telephoned again to Mrs Baker, telling her to get the finished prints of his films, select one complete set from the variants which she would find in the envelope, and mail it to him at Mrs Gunn's.

He returned to No. 48. The excitement of finding Macfarlane had worn off and he looked forward with boredom to a week-end of profitless watching. He had finished the books which he had brought with him and was reduced to reading *Macbeth*, which he had found in a school-text edition on the single bookshelf in his room.

Then the pattern expanded again and Casson could have cheered.

He was sitting by the window, the Leica with its telephoto lens hooded, focused, and aligned, and was turning over the page at the end of the passage:

> *The raven himself is hoarse*
> *That croaks the fatal entrance of Duncan*
> *Under my battlements. Come, you spirits . . .*

when the front door of Perry's house opened. For a moment Casson stared in surprise at the figure which emerged. It was Perry. It wasn't Perry. He leapt for the camera.

The figure bent to lock the front door and turned. Casson clocked the shutter and wound on the film. The figure put on his hat and looked up at the sky. Casson got another photograph. The figure was off down the street, walking fast and purposefully.

It was Perry. It was Bagot. Two in one. Perry had gone into the house with his shopping bag. Bagot had come out. He had come out in the worn mackintosh described by Henry Lockyer. In the moment when he straightened up from locking the door, and before he put on the green pork-pie hat described by Miss Martin of Hatfield, Casson had seen that his hair was darker than usual, dark, glossy, and parted in the middle.

Hurriedly Casson locked away the camera with its precious film, leant out of the window to see if Perry was far enough up the street for pursuit to be safe, and let himself out of the house.

60

The gods had been good to him and no moment of their goodness must be lost. The metamorphosis had happened. Perry had turned into Bagot, and Bagot was on the hunt.

Chapter Six

PERRY took the Underground to Knightsbridge. Casson followed him. One thing only worried him. Where were the heavy horn-rimmed spectacles which had been described both by Lockyer and Miss Martin?

His answer came at Gloucester Road. Almost absent-mindedly Perry took off his usual spectacles, put them in the breast pocket of his suit, and replaced them by heavier and horn-rimmed ones. The transformation was complete. Casson understood.

Of course Perry would not wear them when he left his house and walked up Bickersteth Street. A neighbour might notice them and comment. They would not notice his mackintosh and his green hat. They were common currency in clothing. Nor would they comment on his unusually parted hair for that was hidden by the hat and was, anyway, only designed for the attention of his victim. But the spectacles they would observe.

In the train Perry took no precautions to see if he were being followed. But, once the two men had emerged from Knights-bridge Underground, his tactics changed. He walked aimlessly down streets and round squares, most of them comparatively un-frequented on this Saturday morning. He avoided thoroughfares. He walked down Hans Crescent into Hans Place, circled the Place once, walked across Pont Street into Cadogan Square, went right round the Square, then up Lennox Gardens and Ovington Square, across into the Brompton Road. He turned north up Montpelier Street. Occasionally he glanced behind him.

In Montpelier Square he seemed to have found the hub of his wanderings. Slowly he walked twice round the Square. He took a circuit round by a back street to the south, returned into the Square, made another circuit up Montpelier Walk to the west and back again into the Square. Then he stood for some time on the corner of Montpelier Square and Montpelier Street, stroking his chin, apparently lost in thought.

By the time Perry had reached immobility, Casson was sweating. It was a sultry day, one which had lost its sunlight and become the colour of a dove, and he had had to cover three times the ground that Perry had traced. He dared not be noticed, and he had had to make detours up side streets, circle round to come back from another direction on the suspicious little man: or from the opening of some Mews observe him crossing the intersection of a street, gauge his direction and speed, and circle round again to catch another glimpse of him.

Fortunately he had once lived in Cheval Place and he knew the neighbourhood inside out. After the three quarters of an hour during which Perry wandered and twisted and turned, Casson was sure that he himself had not been observed.

While Perry stood in apparent thought on the corner of Montpelier Square, Casson walked down to the Brompton Road. He picked up a taxi, told it to drive to another corner of the Square, and wait. He sat well back inside it, lost in the darkness, watching. Perry's object was a house on the south side of the Square but which it was Casson could not tell.

At two o'clock Perry left and walked to a snack bar in the Brompton Road. He was there for half an hour, then returned to his post, this time at another corner of the Square. With some reluctance, but because there was nothing else to do, Casson repeated his taxi trick, but this time having it parked in another position; and to lull any suspicion, he told the taxi driver to pretend to be mending the engine, a trick that would work so long as other, and helpful taxi drivers did not come to the rescue of their apparently disabled colleague.

At half past four Perry left again and walked to the Knightsbridge Underground, taking no precautions to see if he were followed. When he disappeared down the steps to the trains, Casson let him go. He was prepared to bet that Perry would return to Bickersteth Street and he was satisfied with the afternoon's work. He had proved to himself that Perry was the blackmailer. All he had to do now was to be able to prove it to Strutt.

He went to his flat in Mount Street and had a bath. While he lay and soaked he thought out the next moves. For some days Perry would watch his prey. Then, when he was sure of his ground, he would pounce. In the meantime Casson must get recognizable photographs of him in his disguise as Bagot; and he must continue to watch him at work in Montpelier Square. The latter was, perhaps, the most difficult task.

When he had dressed and mixed himself a Martini, he rang the garage which maintained the Rolls. He instructed them to drive her at eleven the next morning to Montpelier Square and park her outside a certain house whose number he gave them. On the way they were to pick up his housekeeper.

Mrs Baker was to wait there for him, sitting in the front passenger seat where she could easily be seen by any passer-by such as Perry. Casson would join her later.

The next morning the departure from Bickersteth Street was repeated. Bagot emerged from Perry's house, locked the door, looked up at the sky, put on his green pork-pie hat, and walked away. Casson, waiting and ready, got three photographs. He made no haste to follow the raincoated figure. In the darkened bathroom he wound on the film in the camera, took out the full spool, and sealed it in a canister. He reloaded the camera and took it back into the bedroom, where he put it, together with its telephoto lens and folded tripod, in his suitcase. He labelled the full canister of film with the number, the date, and the time of photography. Then he went up to Mount Street.

He changed into another suit – one that Perry could not yet have seen him wearing. He took a taxi down to Knightsbridge and strolled from the top of Trevor Place to Montpelier Square. The Rolls was parked with Mrs Baker sitting placidly in the front seat, knitting.

He got in. At the far end of the south side of the Square was Perry. This time he was sitting on the kerb with a sketching-block on his knee and a pencil poised in his hand.

Casson sat and chatted to Mrs Baker, telling her the developments on the Perry story. Then he changed his position, moving to the back seat of the car, where he could hardly be seen from outside.

It seemed hours while they waited, but at last, at two o'clock, as on the day before, Perry got up and walked towards Montpelier Street. Presumably he was going to have his snack.

Casson crouched into the cushions at the back of the car. Mrs

Baker kept him informed of Perry's progress. After the little man had disappeared into the Brompton Road, Casson got into the driving-seat and drove back to Mount Street.

Mrs Baker went straight into the kitchen to get him a cold lunch and mix him a salad.

After lunch, properly accompanied by a glass of Vouvray, he went to the telephone again. He knew that Nigel Willington's lawyer lived somewhere near Montpelier Square, and thought that he could get the key of the Square gardens. With some amusement Nigel promised to try and get it.

One point which continued to worry Casson was the identity of Perry's intended victim. If only he could deduce that, he could lay a trap for Perry and catch him in the act of blackmail. He pondered about this for some time. Finally he rang Strutt at his home.

He just got him before the policeman went out for his Sunday afternoon walk across Putney Bridge and along the tow-path. Casson asked him to get the names of all the residents on the south side of the Square.

'I'll do what I can,' said Strutt. 'When do you want them?'

'Tomorrow,' Casson replied. 'Come and dine with me tomorrow evening and bring them along. I'll have the rest of the case tied up by then. . . .'

'We can't act before tomorrow?'

'No. We have no evidence. It may be the wrong man. You'd hate that.'

'Yes. But I'd hate more to lose him, the rat. Who is he?'

'I'll tell you tomorrow. Come along at six thirty.'

'You come here. Adeline˙would like to see you again. God knows why.'

'She's probably bored with policemen,' Casson retorted. 'All right. Six thirty tomorrow. One other thing. Will you bring along the report in the Greenhaugh case?'

'Surely. I'll bring you a bloodhound too. And a season ticket to the Black Museum.' He rang off.

Casson picked up the firm's delivery van from the lock-up which it shared with his own car and drove it down to Montpelier Square. He parked it with its back towards Perry and watched him in the driving-mirror. Perry continued with his sketching.

At five o'clock he got to his feet, shut his sketch-book, took off his spectacles to wipe his face but hurriedly replaced them. He started walking towards the van. Casson scrambled into the back and lay on the dusty floor, wedged up against the side. Even if he glanced in, Perry would see no one: not unless he stopped and had a good look inside.

The passing feet never slackened their pace. Casson gave him three minutes by his watch to get out of sight and then drove off himself. He took the van back to its garage and returned to Mount Street.

He changed back into his Bickersteth Street suit and wrote a note. This he gave to Mrs Baker together with the canister of film. He told her to deliver it first thing next morning to the man who ran the particular studio which developed and enlarged most of his photographs. He wanted it developed in two baths, like the earlier films, and each negative blown up as large as it would go without blurring. He wanted each print numbered with the date and numeral of its parent canister, and he wanted the whole lot by tea-time the same day. It was a rush job, urgent.

In Bickersteth Street he had supper and sat down to write. It would be wrong to follow Perry to the pub that evening. He did not wish, by showing himself again in the Shepley Arms, to re-mind Perry of his face. If the same face were noticed in Montpelier Square, Perry could take fright.

Casson sat up till three in the morning, writing the history of the case – in sequence and in detail. When he had finished and had read through the result, which pleased him, he leant out of the window, smoking a last cigarette.

Bickersteth Street was silent and dim under an edge of moon. A ragged breeze lisped without conviction in the leaves of the only tree in the street, a large, overgrown lilac-bush in the garden of No. 37. The windows which reflected the moonlight were like lid-less eyes afflicted with ophthalmia. He stubbed out his cigarette, locked his written case-history in his suitcase, and went to bed.

He did not wait for Perry the next morning but left the house after breakfast and went to Mount Street, taking the history with him. He changed into yet another suit, took a raincoat and umbrella, got out the Rolls, and drove to Knightsbridge. He parked the car in Raphael Street, well away from Montpelier Square.

His purpose was to keep walking, passing the southern end of the Square at twenty-minute intervals in order to keep a regular check on Perry's presence. The first time he passed, the Square was empty; the second time Perry was there, settled down to his sketching: and he remained in that position throughout the morning.

Casson knocked off at lunch-time for half an hour, then resumed his patrol. He got his raincoat out of the car, thankful for the extra disguise, even though the squalling showers which came down increased his discomfort and irritation. Each time he passed, Perry was sheltering under a thorn tree, reading a newspaper.

Casson realized that he was wasting his time. Perry would not move in for the kill that day: almost certainly not. Nor would he give any indication of the house where his victim unconsciously waited for him. But Casson's obstinacy would not let him relax and he kept up his pacing until Perry disappeared. Thoroughly disgruntled, he went home to his flat.

He had a bath and, while he lay in it, he sipped a large whisky. He changed back into his old suit and went into the library to examine the finished photographs. Deliberately he had put off this moment. So much turned on it.

His lethargy evaporated. Three of the pictures were no good. Perry had been caught in the moment of action and his features were either hidden or blurred. But two were excellent.

One was of Perry dressed as Perry, the other of Perry dressed as Bagot. In both the little man was standing outside the front door of his house and, as luck would have it and because it was a corner house, the name of the street was low on the edge of the picture.

Casson called Mrs Baker into the room and laid the pictures on the table.

'You remember the man we watched in Montpelier Square?' She nodded. 'Do you recognize him here?' She looked at the photographs, discarded that of Perry in his ordinary clothes, hesitated over Perry dressed as Bagot.

'I think this is him, Mr Casson, but I couldn't quite swear to it in a Court of Law, sir.'

'Thank you, Mrs Baker.'

When she had left the room he picked up a pencil from his desk and bent over the photograph of Perry dressed as Bagot. He worked carefully, intently, for a quarter of an hour. Then he called her back. He gestured to the photograph which he had propped against a vase, its back to the window.

'Try this one, Mrs Baker. Not too near.'

She took one look.

'That's him, sir.' Her voice was contented. She liked to see her Mr Casson happy. He was happy. All he had done was faintly to pencil in heavier-rimmed spectacles than those which Perry had worn when he had emerged from his house and been photographed.

Casson scribbled a name and telephone number on a pad and threw it across to Mrs Baker.

'Ring this, would you, and tell Nevill to wait till I get there? I'll be ten minutes.' He was out of the door, leaving it swinging behind him, and down the stairs three at a time, scorning the slowness of the lift. He almost ran up Carlos Place past the Connaught Hotel, along Adams Row, across Davies Street, and down Grosvenor Hill. He pushed open the door of the photographic studio and went straight through the waiting-room into the inner office.

'Nevill, I want you to do me an urgent job,' he said. The pale young man with the bow-tie pushed back his chair and waved petulantly.

'Oh, my dear,' he said, 'not again. I did one for you this morning. It's too much. Really, it is.'

'Never mind,' said Casson. 'You're the only man in town who can do it.' To some extent it was true. Nevill had an affected voice but he was a brilliant photographer. At Casson's words his expression softened.

'Very well,' he said. 'What is it?'

Casson pushed the photograph over to him.

'Fake this,' he said. 'Re-touch it and re-take it so that the specs come out real.'

68

Nevill regarded it distastefully.

'Not very pretty, dear, is he?' he remarked. 'When do you want it?'

'Dawn tomorrow. Six copies. Whole-plate size. At my flat.'

'Oh no. . . .'

'Double overtime charges,' said Casson, making for the door. 'It's a matter of someone's sanity. I know you won't fail me. So long, cocky.' He dodged out of the studio and was half-way down the street before Nevill could have summoned the energy for a further protest.

He rang Strutt from his flat and said he would be late. He collected two sets of the untouched photographs, the key of Montpelier Square Gardens which Nigel had sent round in an envelope, the written history of the Perry case, and set off for Fulham.

Strutt lived in a spacious, old-fashioned flat in Bishop's Park Road, Fulham, overlooking tennis-courts and trees. He greeted Casson with a twinkle in his piggy eyes, eagerly taking the big envelope from under his guest's arm.

'Not till later,' said Casson. 'We'll look at them then.'

'You got him?'

'I think so.'

'Good boy. Good boy. Here's Adeline.'

Mrs Strutt was forty and looked twenty-seven. Her complexion was still that of a girl's, her heavy gold hair untouched by grey, her eyes blue, calm, untroubled. She looked a happy woman. A pity, thought Casson, that she could not have had more children, girls for preference. But she had nearly died giving birth to their one son, Alan, Casson's godchild.

Casson was a favourite of hers and she was so obviously glad to see him that he was touched. They had a vast meal, during which Casson, relaxed, drank a lot of whisky. Strutt drank his lager, Adeline water.

'Didn't get you wine,' said Strutt, heaping the roast potatoes on his plate with satisfaction. 'Don't know anything about the stuff. Better for you to drink whisky.'

They discussed the future of Alan, whom Strutt hoped would go to King's School, Canterbury.

'Clever little devil,' Strutt grunted.

'What's he going to be?' Casson asked.

'Don't know. Too clever to be a copper.' Adeline smiled in amused admiration of her husband. Casson agreed with her, having considerable respect for the intelligence of the Metropolitan Police.

'Better let me make him a wine merchant,' Casson suggested. Adeline gave him a quick glance and began to clear away the red-and-white patterned plates.

'You men will want to gossip,' she said. 'I'll call you later when I've made the tea.' Casson shuddered.

'Come along,' said Strutt, grabbing his arm. 'We'll go into the den.'

The den was a long slot off the dining-room. It was littered with cricket bats, pads, bursting boxes of microscope slides, and piles of newspapers. Strutt sank into an ancient wickerwork armchair.

'Now,' he said. 'Talk.'

Casson gave him the written case-history. Strutt read it through twice, saying nothing. He reached for the photographs and studied them.

'Good,' he commented. 'But not proof.'

'I get that tomorrow morning.' Strutt took a swig of lager and looked at him. 'On that photograph' – Casson pointed at the one of Perry emerging from his house as Bagot – 'I pencilled in heavier spectacles. I showed it to my housekeeper, who watched him with me yesterday in Montpelier Square. She identified it at once. I'm having it faked up and six copies made. I shall take one early tomorrow and show it to Lockyer. If he identifies it we have proof. Perry will be Bagot.'

'Lockyer won't play,' Strutt objected.

'He will.'

'Why? He's frightened.'

'Gamman's Bank. Let me see the report on Greenhaugh.' Casson leafed over the papers. He skimmed down the page and then pointed. 'See? I thought it would be. Greenhaugh's principal Bank in London was Gamman's. That's where his main account was kept. He only had an arrangement with the Lloyd's Branch in Mayfair because it was near his office. Lockyer of course banks at Gamman's. Macfarlane works in Gamman's. Lockyer will have to play because it looks as if one of his staff is giving information to a blackmailer. I'm sure that's how Perry got his background stuff – and how he knew exactly how much to tap them for. . . .'

'Macfarlane's the stooge?'

'It looks like it.'

Strutt's eyes were bulging.

'Good,' he said. 'I'd like copies of your faked-up picture of Perry. I'll send one down to the Yard and one to the Hatfield boys for Miss Martin to identify. You'll let me know about Lockyer?'

'As soon as I've seen him. Say, ten thirty tomorrow morning. I'll ring you.'

'Right. Now: how do we catch Perry?'

'Let's have a look at the people who live in Montpelier Square.' Strutt produced the list. After a minute Casson threw it back at him.

'Useless. Lawyers, doctors, civil servants, stockbrokers. All respectable. Each one a potential victim. None outstandingly suited. So we can't warn the victim and set a trap in his house.'

'We could pick up Perry as he makes the touch and try to frighten him?'

'No good. He wouldn't squeak. Nor would the victim. You know that.'

'Blast them.'

'We must go on watching him. Let's hope he gives some indication of the victim. Then we might try a trap.'

'Shall I put our boys on to watching him?'

'No,' said Casson quickly. 'It's bad enough with me. There's no room for another. He'd smell trouble and then you've lost this chance.'

'Yes,' Strutt replied grudgingly. 'All right.'

Adeline came in with tea for herself and her husband and another whisky for Casson. She perched on the rickety table in the window while they drank and chatted and Casson was persuaded to tell her once again, with gestures, the story of how he and Strutt had first met at the beginning of the war. Casson was on leave and had been amusing himself at a chemmy game. Strutt had been in charge of the raiding party. Casson had protested vigorously, accused Strutt of being a Puritan blockhead, and lectured him on what he considered to be the proper duties of the Police. Casson had been fined five pounds as a frequenter and had then taken Strutt to lunch. The lunch finished at a quarter to four that afternoon. Since then they had been firm and argumentative friends.

Casson left at midnight and went back to Chiswick.

'Extraordinary,' said Adeline, after he had gone. 'Why does he do it?'

'Do what, love?'

'Hunt criminals.'

'He likes it,' replied her husband. 'So do I.'

'But why?'

'We like people, I suppose.'

'But not criminals?'

'They're people. Besides, he's got a conscience.'

Adeline smiled and collected the teacups.

'Have you?' she asked. Her husband grinned.

'Lord, no. I'm too busy.'

'You're too callous?' she suggested, sitting precariously on the arm of his chair.

'That's right,' he replied. 'Now, it's bed for you, my love, or you'll get wrinkles round the eyes.'

'Poor Casson,' she said. 'Once he gets into a thing like that, it sort of eats him. You know. He gets all tied up inside and angry. Not like you.'

'Not like me,' Strutt agreed, kissing her. 'Now come along.'

Casson was up early the next morning and away to Mount Street, leaving a note for Mrs Gunn to explain his unusual departure. At Mount Street he had breakfast and waited for the finished photographs to arrive.

They were delivered at ten minutes past nine. Casson ripped open the envelope, glanced at them, and laughed. Nevill had done his work well. Bagot stood there to the life.

He sealed two of the portraits in an envelope, addressed it to Strutt, and left it at the West End Central Police Station. He arrived in Launceston Street at a quarter to ten, in time, he reckoned, to catch Henry Lockyer before he went to the City. He was shown into the sitting-room.

Lockyer was standing by the fireplace, looking hostile. Casson took the photograph from its covering and laid it on the table.

'Who's that?' he asked. Lockyer stared at him coldly, hesitated, walked over to the table. For five or six seconds he looked at the photograph, then walked back to the fireplace.

'It could be him,' he said in an unemotional voice.

'Who?' Casson persisted.

'Bagot. And now that you have got your answer, I fear that I must leave you. I am going to the City. Can I offer you a lift?'

He walked over to a side-table and took a cigarette from a highly-polished wooden box. His face was turned half-way from Casson as he lit it but Casson could see the unsteady fingers which held the match.

'I am sorry,' said Casson, 'but I am afraid I cannot go yet.' Lockyer threw the scarcely-smoked cigarette in the fireplace and rounded on him.

'I have told you that I do not desire to proceed further in this affair,' he said, and there was an inflexion of desperate anger in his tone. 'I wish you to respect my confidences. I regard the whole matter as closed.'

'I am forced to tell you,' said Casson, 'that you cannot consider it as closed. . . .'

'It's nothing to do with you. It is my affair. I prefer to forget it.'

'You can't. Your bank is involved.'

Lockyer stared at him.

'Gamman's?' he asked harshly. 'How?'

'Bagot gets his information from your bank.'

Lockyer was silent. In the end he turned away.

'I don't believe it,' he said.

'I'm pretty sure I'm right,' Casson was beginning when Lockyer's man came into the room and announced that the taxi was at the door.

'Right, Dobbie,' said the banker. 'I will be there in a minute.' He waited until his man had closed the door, then turned on Casson. 'Pretty sure!' he remarked bitterly. 'Pretty sure! You'd

73

better start being certain before you make accusations like that.'

Casson sat down on the arm of a chair.

'Bagot blackmailed a man before you,' he said quietly, 'and that man banked at Gamman's. As a matter of incidental interest he committed suicide.' Lockyer's mouth twitched. 'Your own affairs,' Casson continued, 'are known in Gamman's, especially the secret of your Boys' Clubs. You have identified the Bagot who blackmailed you, and that same Bagot is a friend of a man who works in your bank.'

Lockyer shrugged.

'Coincidence.'

'Bagot is going to blackmail another man some time this week,' Casson went on. 'I will bet you a pound that the new victim banks at Gamman's.'

'You know who this Bagot is?' Lockyer shot the question at him.

'Oh, yes,' Casson replied in a casual tone. 'I know who he is.'

Lockyer opened his mouth, shut it again, then asked:

'Who is his friend in my Bank?'

'A young man named Macfarlane.'

'What?' Casson was surprised by the force of the response. 'Say that again.'

'Macfarlane. One of the tellers. Young, fair-haired chap of about thirty.'

'Jim Macfarlane,' Lockyer breathed the words. 'It can't be. I won't believe it.'

'Why not?'

'He's a fine young fellow. Very promising. A first-rate yachtsman.'

Casson sighed to himself. When would the English learn that a pleasant face and an aptitude for sport were not automatic guarantees of honesty?

'Well, there it is,' he said, rising to his feet and putting the photograph of Bagot back into its covering. 'I suppose you wouldn't give me Macfarlane's particulars?'

'Certainly not. I'm a banker.'

'Your bank will look a bit shamefaced if one of its tellers is cited in Court as an accessory to blackmail.'

Slowly, carefully, Lockyer sat down. He stretched out his legs and, his face turned downwards, seemed to be engrossed in contemplating his expensive black shoes, turning them first one way, then the other, as if to see that they were properly polished.

'Very well,' he said at length. 'But you understand that I will in no way be brought publicly into this affair?'

'I understand.'

'Right,' He rose to his feet.

'Perhaps you would also see if your bank knows anything about a man called John Perry?' Casson suggested.

'Perry? Why? I've never heard of him.'

'You've met him.'

'Perry? Don't recollect the fellow.'

'You know him as Bagot.'

'Oh,' Lockyer scrutinized him. 'Oh,' he repeated.

'I have an idea that he may have been connected with the bank,' Casson observed. 'Mind you, it's a long shot.'

'Perry. Very well.' Lockyer went straight out of the room and Casson followed him. The banker got into his taxi without another word and was driven off. Casson looked after him, for the first time feeling as sorry for the man as he would feel for any animal caught in a spring trap.

He himself went to Montpelier Square. He would be there by eleven and safely ensconced long before Perry should arrive.

With the key sent him by Nigel Willington, he let himself into the black, wooden shed in the gardens. A taxi came, deposited a passenger and two suitcases, and drove away. A young Nanny wheeled out a full and squalling pram. Women went out shopping. Montpelier Square was normal: except for Bagot. There was no Bagot.

Casson grew more and more restless. Surely Bagot would watch his prey until the moment when he chose to pounce? Surely he would watch and watch and watch? Then where was he?

He did not appear at all, and when Casson returned to his flat at six he was in a high temper. Strutt was sitting in the library, reading a book.

'What do you want?' said Casson. 'A free drink?'

'Yes. What was Bagot doing at Brighton?'

Casson rounded on him.

'What?'

'He spent the day at Brighton.'

'How do you know?'

'We put a man on to him at dawn this morning.'

'You – you bulging cheat of a bogey,' said Casson.

Strutt chuckled.

'Can't be too sure,' he remarked. 'The runt nipped off to Brighton this morning. Took a room at a hotel. Spent the day in his room. Had no lunch. Got back to town an hour ago. What did he do? Why did he do it?'

'I can't imagine.'

'He had no mistress. He had no drink. He had no fun. Why?'

Casson shrugged.

'Sea air.'

'Sea ruddy air my Aunt Twitch.' Strutt snorted and got up out of his chair. 'So long, boy. Thought you'd like to know.' He went away.

Casson puzzled over the incident but in no way did it make sense.

He resumed his watch in the Square the next morning, this time getting into position at half past ten, armed with *Alice in Wonderland* in case his wait was again frustrated. He did not dare follow Perry from Bickersteth Street, for if he did so he could not enter the gardens unobserved. He trusted to Strutt's watch-dog to keep Perry in view until the little man turned into Bagot and reached his hunting ground.

The same baby came out in its pram and was wheeled away. A daily woman slammed a basement door, climbed the steps, and went home. At the noise of another door opening, this time from the south side of the Square, he glanced casually through the grimy window of the shed.

He stood rigid, his heart pounding. Perry was coming out of a house: Perry dressed as Bagot: Perry followed by a woman. Coming out of No. 77.

She shut the door and walked beside Perry down the street. Neither said a word. Once she glanced furtively behind her. On the corner, where the Square joined Montpelier Street, she stopped.

Perry turned to her, and Casson could see his lips moving. She seemed to hesitate, gave another look back, and went on.

As they turned the corner of the Square, Casson ran for the gate. He let himself out and sprinted down the pavement. Before the corner he slowed and strolled sedately into Montpelier Street.

Perry had just hailed a cruising cab. It squealed to a stop and the pair climbed in. As it turned into the Brompton Road, Casson ran again. There was no taxi on the rank. He ran on into the Brompton Road. Swearing profanely he flagged taxi after taxi. They were all taken.

He shrugged and gave it up. The other cab was well out of sight. He had no hope of following it. Bagot had pounced and Casson had failed to net him.

Chapter Seven

DISCONSOLATELY he walked towards Harrod's. The opportunity for which he had worked so hard and so patiently had arrived at ripeness and been snatched away from him. Perry had struck too fast.

Casson had gambled on Perry giving some clue as to the identity of his victim. Then a trap could have been set. Perry would have walked in: politely, offensively self-confident. He would have made his demand. He would have assured his victim that he was too clever to blackmail them for something that they had actually done. So it had been with Lockyer; so it had presumably been with Greenhaugh.

In would have walked Strutt, Perry would have been arrested. The victim, their innocence clearly established by Perry's own words taken down by listening policemen, could not hesitate to give evidence.

That chance was gone. God alone knew when it would recur or how many months it would be before Perry decided to strike again. And Casson would have to give up. He could not possibly go on following Perry for that length of time.

It would even be useless to ring Strutt, tell him to find out the woman's name from his list of residents, and have him ring Gamman's to stop them paying her cheque. The bank – if she did go to Gamman's Head Office – could scarcely refuse to honour it and if Strutt picked up Perry, both he and his victim would refuse to acknowledge that it was blackmail. He continued to walk along the pavement, his head sunk in thought. A small boy, running and looking behind, cannoned into him. Casson nearly lost his balance. His frustration flared up into anger. He gripped the urchin by his bony shoulder and spun him round.

'I've a mind to put you in prison,' he said fiercely.

He let the boy go and strode on. Suddenly his temper dissolved and he laughed at himself. He turned. The urchin was standing there, his finger in his mouth, looking after him.

'Come here, sonny,' he said. The boy hesitated and half-turned to run away. He saw the smile on Casson's face and came doubtfully nearer.

'Here, young fellow,' said Casson, pressing a shilling into the sticky hand. 'Here's a silver penny for you. Hop it and buy a lolly.'

He felt better. He went into a telephone box and rang Strutt. Strutt's voice was eager, exultant.

'The Martin girl identified your photograph,' he said. 'Perry was the runt who followed her about and picked her up. . . .'

'I want you to pull in a taxi and take a statement from the driver,' Casson interrupted. 'Here's the number.'

'What's the matter?' Strutt asked. 'You sound as if you had a hangover.'

'I have,' Casson retorted. 'That taxi took Perry and his victim to a bank. He beat me to it. I lost him.'

'I see.' There was a slight pause at the other end of the line. 'Hard luck, boy.' Strutt's commiseration was clearly sincere. 'Never mind,' he went on. 'We'll get him next time.'

'I doubt it,' answered Casson. 'I'll come in and see you this afternoon.'

He returned to Chiswick and sat down by the window to wait. Nearly an hour after he had got back he saw Perry walking down the street. He was wearing his ordinary spectacles and from his right hand swung a brown-paper carrier-bag such as you can buy in the big stores and fold up and put in your mackintosh pocket.

Casson looked malevolently at the little man. In that paper bag were how many hundreds of pounds? And some wretched woman, who two hours ago had met Perry for the first time in her life, was now the prey to a constant and nagging fear – fear of the next visit – for she would not believe Perry's assurance that he never taxed his victims twice: fear of those dreaded visits whose repetition would stretch into her future and make it purgatory.

Casson went back to Mayfair. Strutt jumped up when he entered the office and pushed out a chair for him.

'The bloodhound's limping,' Casson observed wryly as he sat down. He told Strutt the story, and the fat policeman never interrupted.

'At any rate we know two things,' said Strutt when Casson had finished. 'We know that Martin and Bagot are Perry and we know where Perry lives. You found that out, and it's damn good work – for an amateur,' he added, his little eyes twinkling.

Casson laughed.

'For a male bitch you're a nice one,' he retorted. 'But, look at it how you will,' he went on, 'we've lost our chance. There won't be another one.'

'There'll always be another one. I wonder,' Strutt continued dreamily, 'What would happen if we knocked him off this evening. He'd have the money on him, wouldn't he?'

Casson shook his head.

'You know he'd say that they were his savings.'

'Yes. What about his victim? She might play ball.'

'Who is she?' Strutt pushed across the desk the list of the residents in Montpelier Square.

'No. 77,' said Casson, glancing down the list. 'Mrs Neil Gordonstoun. Lt-General Neil Gordonstoun. A Senior Officer's wife. She's bound to be respectable or Perry wouldn't have picked her. And if she's respectable and a General's wife, she's jolly respectable.'

'I was thinking we might call on her,' said Strutt, undoing a paper clip. Casson shrugged. 'But I was also thinking that you would do it better. The police would frighten her. She wouldn't talk. And we're in a sticky position. We knew she was going to be blackmailed and we never warned her. . . .'

'I didn't know it was her,' Casson broke in.

'She won't understand that. We know so much that we ought to have known all. The police always get blamed.'

'You are undoubtedly a twister,' said Casson. 'You pass the buck?'

'I pass,' Strutt replied woodenly.

Casson laughed. 'Splendid. I want to see her. Come and have a drink?'

'Too early. Now listen,' his voice changed and became brisk. 'We've run the rule over Perry's nark, that young chap in the bank, what's his name?' He picked up a report. 'Macfarlane. James Robert Macfarlane. Known as Jim Macfarlane. Born in

Lockerbie, Dumfriesshire . . . Lieutenant in the Territorial Army. Yes.'

'What a bore,' murmured Casson.

'What's a bore?'

'I persuaded Lockyer this morning to find out about him from the bank.'

Strutt chuckled. 'We're not so slow as we look,' he observed. 'We had him followed from the bank. Lives in a flat in Shaftesbury Avenue. Curious place. I suppose the rent's very low. We'll keep him watched.'

'You won't get much. He will give his information to Perry at that snack bar in the City. And that will be the only time he operates. You might get the name of the next victim – if you're lucky.'

'We'll see,' said Strutt. 'Now. What about Perry? We'd better give him a run-over. I want to dig up his past.'

'Lockyer's finding out if he was ever connected with Gamman's,' said Casson. 'I should leave him until I ring you.'

'Right.' The telephone rang. Strutt listened in silence, grunted, and put it down.

'The taxi-man,' he said. 'They pulled him into the Yard and got a statement from him. He identified the fare from your photograph which I sent down to the Criminal Record Office. He took him and a woman to Gamman's –'

'Of course,' Casson interrupted.

'. . . dropped them there and was paid. He saw the woman go into the bank. The man stayed outside. He drove off. That's all. Now I'd like a formal statement from you about this morning and the photographs and how you found Perry.'

It took Casson over an hour to write it and only Strutt's invective kept him at the task. By the time he had finished he was profoundly bored. It had to be factual. There was no room for metaphors or hyperboles, none of the graces and pirouettes of imaginative writing; and he fervently disliked pedestrian prose which, to him, was like salad without oil and vinegar.

He was exhausted when he had finished and went down to Cane's for a long, cool drink. He took his pint of Pimm's into the smoking-room that faced across St James's Street and searched *Who's Who* for Neil Gordonstoun.

The entry was not very informative. Gordonstoun was a soldier of considerable bravery. To that his decorations bore ample witness. His regiment was a fine one. He had an address in Scotland and another in London – 77 Montpelier Square, sw7. His recreation was given as Stalking. Casson shut the thick red book and smiled. His wife had been well and truly stalked. But he needed more before he went to see her, so he rang up a friend of his in the Adjutant-General's Department.

'Gordonstoun,' said the voice. 'Know him a bit, you know. Extraordinary chap. Why?'

'Friend of mine was asking,' Casson replied glibly. 'I think he wants to get his son into the Army.'

The voice cackled. 'Neil'll chivvy him around all right. Believes in discipline. Amazing chap. Runs a mile before breakfast and won't sit down till luncheon. Says it's bad for the backbone. Jolly old martinet, you know. Reads the lesson in church and all that. Once ticked me off for saying "Damn" before a woman. The troops love him. Just shows, doesn't it?'

'Where's he now?' Casson asked.

'Don't know,' said the voice. 'Wait a minute.' Casson heard the voice shout 'Johnny!' and then mumble.

'Kenya,' said the voice in triumph. 'Limbering up the Empire. Teaching our black brothers to play bridge. Good show.'

'What's the matter with you, Dick?' Casson asked petulantly. 'Are you tight?'

'Not a bit, old boy. Sober and hard-working officer. Just had a ten-to-one on a gee-gee. A quid on the kisser and won by a length.'

'Splendid,' said Casson and brought the conversation back to its lost point. 'Do you know Gordonstoun's wife?'

'No. Never heard tell. So she can't be fast and she can't be a whizzer. If she was I'd have heard. It'd get around. The grapevine system you know.'

'Thanks a lot, Dickie. . . .'

'I've got a tip for next week,' said the voice. 'Make a note of it. A quid on the snout and you'll be rich. Don't say I told you.'

Patiently Casson made the noises of a man taking down a hot tip from a friend and rang off. Perry was a good picker. The wife of an absent and martinet General was in no position to withstand a clever blackmail. But, so far as he knew, she was Perry's first woman victim. Therefore, he might have said something *gauche*, something that made her hate him more than fear him. She might have a conscience. She might even help. You never knew with women. That is why Casson liked them.

Chapter Eight

AT Mount Street there was a note from Lockyer which had been brought by hand. There was nothing new about Macfarlane but there were fresh details on Perry.

John Henry Perry had entered Gamman's Bank in 1921 at the age of seventeen. His career in the bank had been undistinguished. After thirty years' service he had retired. He was then unmarried and his address had been 17 Elgar Crescent, w2. A postscript added: 'No war service.'

One point puzzled Casson. How had Perry dared to blackmail clients of the bank in which he himself had worked for so long? He must have reckoned that they might recognize him, even under his disguise. Unless he had been one of the unseen workers behind the frosted glass wall which separated the public from the private side of the bank, a discreetly hidden and discreetly humming hive into which even Lockyer might not bother to penetrate.

Casson copied out the particulars and sent them to Strutt. Then he returned to Chiswick. It would not do for him to be absent from the Shepley Arms on the day when Perry had made his pounce.

Perry was punctual. He drank his pint slowly and left at his usual time. Casson leant on the bar, talking about the neighbourhood to Peter, keeping his back to the blackmailer.

He no longer worried about following Perry in the daytime. The blackmailer would not prepare for another *coup* for some weeks, perhaps even for some months. Instead of staying in Hammersmith, Casson went up to his office the next morning and dealt with an accumulation of correspondence. At midday he rang Mrs Gordonstoun. He asked if he could come to see her, gave the name of his firm, and said that he wanted to see her about some business in which her husband was interested. Her voice was cool and pleasant but distant. She sounded an essentially nice woman. She asked him to tea.

He drove the Rolls to Montpelier Square and parked it outside the door of No. 77 so that its bonnet could be seen from the drawing-room window. A young maid with a pert look opened the door and showed him into the long double drawing-room.

Mrs Gordonstoun was a woman of about thirty-eight. A honey blonde, observed Casson, who only really liked dark brunettes and red-haired girls. Her ankles are bad, he added, as she rose from the sofa to greet him. He took in the string of real pearls, the smart, but not startling, print dress, the unobtrusive pink nail varnish, and the leather London shoes.

'How do you do, Mr Duker,' she said. 'I am afraid my husband is away and I don't know if I can be of much help.'

'In Kenya, isn't he?' Casson replied. 'I am sure you can help, Mrs Gordonstoun.'

She sat down while Casson lit a cigarette, then, with an apology, offered her one, which she refused. He put down on a table the covered photograph of Perry which he had brought with him.

'Before I begin I would like to tell you who I am,' he said. She lifted one hand in a slight gesture.

'I am sure, Mr Duker, that it is not necessary.'

'I am the Director of Manton and Heywood in Vigo Street,' he went on, not heeding her. 'I was a Captain in the Airborne Division at the end of the war. I am a member of Cane's. . . .'

She stood up. 'Please, Mr Duker,' she protested. 'I am sure I don't need to know all this. . . .'

'I think you do,' he replied. 'In a minute you will need to know that I am a normal – that is to say a fairly normal – and respectable citizen. You see, I have an odd hobby. I am interested in the unusual behaviour of my fellow citizens. Of blackmailers, for example.'

She had been playing with the string of pearls round her throat. Her hand clenched on the pale string and twisted it. Her face was set but she could not hide the fear in her eyes.

'Mr Duker,' she said firmly. 'I do not know why you have come here. If it is some business of my husband's, please tell me what it is. I do not understand why you should tell me that you are interested in blackmail. I know nothing about it.'

Casson took no notice.

'Mrs Gordonstoun,' he said, 'an acquaintance of mine was

85

blackmailed some weeks ago. I shall not, of course, tell you his name, in the same way that I shall not disclose yours to him. I promised to help him. I think you can help me and I think I can be of value to you. . . .'

'Are you a policeman?' she asked quickly.

'No. I am a wine merchant.'

'What did you say your firm was?'

'Manton, Heywood and Partner. In Vigo Street.'

She picked up a telephone directory and flipped over the pages. She dialled a number. Casson watched her, amused. She spoke into the phone, then gestured to Casson. 'There is an extension in the hall. Please speak to the firm yourself. I shall listen in.'

Casson spoke to Tippett and put down the receiver. She came back into the room.

'I apologize,' she said. 'If you come into my house with a series of – peculiar statements, you must expect me to find out if you really exist. I think we had better have some tea.' She rang for the maid. 'I find that tea is the sanest of drinks,' she observed to him, with a faint smile. Casson forebore to contradict her, although all he wanted was a glass of cold hock.

She made conversation while the tea was brought in on its trolley. She poured for him and offered him a sandwich, which he felt it only diplomatic to take. Then she sat down, stirring her teaspoon round and round in her cup.

Casson reached behind him for the photograph of Perry dressed as Bagot, uncovered it, and laid it on the sofa beside her.

'At twenty-five minutes to eleven yesterday morning that man in the photograph blackmailed you,' he said.

She laid her teaspoon carefully in the saucer of her cup and was about to speak. But Casson forestalled her.

'If you will forgive me,' he said, 'I would like to tell you all I know. It may make it easier for you to tell me the little I do not know. First of all, please look at that photograph.'

She glanced at it, then quickly away again. But, as though drawn to it by an ashamed fascination, she glanced back, kept her gaze on it for a few moments. Then she looked steadily at Casson.

'Well?' she said without emotion. Casson marvelled again at

the quality of implacable reserve that manifested itself so instinctively in the embarrassed Englishman or outraged Englishwoman.

'The man in that photograph is called Perry,' he went on. 'He lives in London. He is unmarried. I know for a certainty that he has blackmailed three people. For his first victim he used the name of Martin. His victim committed suicide. For the second *coup* he used a second name: false again, of course. His second victim is still alive and will remain alive for at least twenty years. That means two decades of fear in case the blackmailer strikes again. You are the third victim, and with you he will have used yet another false name. I do not know what it is. . . .'

He paused, hoping that she would automatically answer his question and thus commit herself. She said nothing.

'In the first two cases which I have mentioned,' he went on, 'Perry blackmailed his victims for things which they had not done.' Her eyelids flickered. 'When he blackmailed you at twenty-five to eleven yesterday morning he blackmailed you also for something which you had not done; but he located his mythical incident at a time and in a place when you could have done it. More than that, it was in a place the nature of which makes it impossible for you ever to disprove his accusation. Am I right?'

She poured herself some more tea and forgot to offer any to him.

'You know so much, Mr Duker, that I am sure you must be right,' she replied evenly. Casson persevered.

'Perry pointed out to you that if you did not pay what he demanded he would see to it that the authorities, or your husband' – again her eyes flickered, and with satisfaction Casson noticed this second tremor of admission – 'or someone dear to you would be made aware of your alleged indiscretion. He explained to you that you dare not take this risk because you could never disprove the allegation. He pointed out that, for the same reason, you would not dare take him to Court. He promised you that he would never visit you again, reassuring you with his theory that the clever criminal never milks the same victim twice. He then suggested that you should accompany him to Gamman's Bank, where you have your account; that you should draw a sum of money from the bank in pound notes – a sum you could just afford without gravely inconveniencing yourself, and, for example, without declaring it to your husband – and that you should hand it to him in the street outside the bank. When you had done that he disappeared.'

She put down her teacup.

'You knew he was going to ... to do this?' Casson did not reply. 'Why did you not have him arrested?' she went on.

Casson spread out his hands in a gesture of confession.

'I failed ...' he began.

'Failed?' she said, her voice rising slightly. 'Yes, indeed. You failed to warn me. You allowed me to be blackmailed. You let me be put in a position from which I can never extricate myself. You let me brand myself guilty of something I had never done. All because you were careless enough to fail!'

The sudden animation, the release of energy in her voice, her flushed cheeks, and the bitter anger in her eyes removed her at once from the orbit of military respectability and made her a warm, vibrating, ordinary, and unofficial woman. She was quite attractive, Casson thought.

'I did not know that much,' he explained. 'I knew Perry had selected a victim on this side of the Square. ...'

'But you must have known who it was. ...'

'No. ...'

'Then how did you know that he had chosen this side of the Square?'

'I followed him, Mrs Gordonstoun. I followed him night and day.' Casson laced his tone of voice with all the acid he could muster.

'Oh,' she said. 'I see. I am sorry.'

'I had hoped,' he continued, 'to get from him some indication of his victim's identity, to warn the victim, and to trap Perry as he pounced. I can only apologize for my failure.'

'Why have you done all this, Mr Duker? It is normally a matter for the police.'

'Some men collect postage stamps,' he replied. 'Some spend their holidays hunting for *cypridium* in Continental woods. Some, like your husband, stalk stags. I collect those human beings who mince along the fringes of illegality. And I collect them, Mrs

Gordonstoun, because it is then that their behaviour is least inhibited and most human.'

'It must be an amusing game,' she observed coldly.

Casson had intended to provoke this reaction.

'In this case,' he went on, his voice deliberately flippant, 'I am hunting the man Perry since one man has died and another goes in fear, and a woman, even a brave woman like yourself, Mrs Gordonstoun, will have nightmares: all because Perry exists and is greedy.'

'Yes,' she answered, speaking very softly, as though to herself. 'Yes. Naturally.' She looked up at him. 'I am sorry for your sake that you failed to trap Mr Perry,' she said.

Casson smiled.

'I didn't fail.'

She leant forward, her face a shade paler.

'But you said . . . you mean you're going to arrest him? And bring him into a Court?'

'Do you agree with me, Mrs Gordonstoun, that Perry is a menace to decent people?'

'Of course.'

'And that he should be sent to prison?'

'Yes.'

'Well, I can do that.'

'How?'

'With your help.'

'Oh.' She sat back, her hand going once again to play with the string of pearls round her throat.

'You can give evidence against him. That evidence will send him to gaol. Your name will never be mentioned in Court. Will you help?'

'Certainly not.'

'Why not, Mrs Gordonstoun?'

She picked up the teapot, put it down again.

'When Fenton came here yesterday. . . .'

'Fenton?'

She indicated the photograph of Bagot which lay on the sofa beside her.

'This man. He said his name was Fenton. He had the . . . the

89

impertinence to suggest to me that I was friendly . . . that I was
. . . that I was having an *affaire* with a Captain in my husband's
regiment. He named the day when Willy –'

'Willy?'

'The Captain. When he took me out to lunch. We went to the
cinema and came back here to dine. He stayed the night before
going back to York. He is an old friend. I have known him since
childhood. Fenton told me the time when we left this house, the
restaurant and the film we went to, the time we returned. He
knew the time Willy left the next morning and the number of his
car which he had left in the Square. He suggested that my husband would not be pleased to learn of this . . . this *affaire*.' She
made a grimace. 'The way in which he spoke the word was revolting. He was prim. Yet he took delight in using the word.'

'Surely . . .' Casson began but she hurried on.

'Some time ago I gave Willy money. It was to get him out of
a – out of an entanglement with a woman of whom I thoroughly
disapproved and who was certain to let him down. Fenton knew
that I had given him this money. That, he said, would only rein-
force my husband's distress.'

'But your husband would never believe this rigmarole. It's a
cheap novelette: stuff for the sillier housemaids.'

'Are you married, Mr Duker?' He shook his head and she
appeared to muse, absent-mindedly removing her rings and placing them on the tea-tray. When she spoke again he was startled
by the cold sincerity in her voice.

'Marriage is a curious experience, Mr Duker. It teaches you
many things. It teaches you, for example, that life is a mixture
of' – she hesitated for a second – 'of love and discipline and
pettiness. You say that Fenton's threat was fit only for a cheap
novelette. So it was. But there is a part of everybody's mind which
yearns to believe in cheap novelettes, in music under the moon,
in handsome heroes, in masked intrigue and love triumphant. It
is trash and it is untrue, and that is why people believe it. The
housemaid's mind, Mr Duker, is more common than perhaps you
know.

'Neil, my husband,' she went on, 'is a good man. He is what
my grandfather would have called an upright man. I know him

very well and I am very fond of him. He is devoted to me. He is also devoted to his principles.

'All husbands, Mr Duker, are jealous. So, I have no doubt' – she smiled fleetingly – 'are all women. It is natural. Neil might not believe this absurd accusation: but it would stick in his mind. And that is why I will not, under any circumstances whatsoever, give evidence against your blackmailer.'

Casson was silent.

'In four months' time,' he said at length, 'someone else will be blackmailed. It may be a young girl. She may take an overdose of aspirin. She might have been your daughter.'

'She might, Mr Duker. But I have no daughter and I do have a husband. You will forgive me if I protect what I have.'

There was nothing that he could say. She seemed disinclined to talk further. He rose and took his leave. As he shook her hand she smiled wanly and said:

'I wish you luck, Mr Duker. You understand, of course, that everything I have said is in confidence?'

He bowed his head in assent, recollecting the ancient Greek adage that an oath not spoken in the heart is not an oath at all. He offered up a brief and hidden memorandum to the Gods to forgive him his falseness and Mrs Gordonstoun her frailty.

The sunlight in the Square seemed false and hectic, too lavishly flushed with gold for the early hour of evening. It was like a pre-Raphaelite painter trying to copy Botticelli while all the time he thought about drugs instead of cherubim. Casson shivered. The worm that was Perry was eating into him. He felt ill at ease, soiled, unhappy, miserably and fruitlessly angry.

He drove to the West End Central Police Station. Strutt was out. He waited impatiently, his mind unable to ignore the complicated equation of pain that was circling inside it, a computation of past and potential agony, a subtraction and addition of misery which refused to be solved. On the one side were Perry's past, and on the other were his future, victims. Which must he, Casson Duker, jettison to save the other?

Strutt looked tired when he came in. Together and without speaking they went up to the Superintendent's office. Still in silence they sat down, one either side of the desk. Strutt fished around in the top drawer for a paper-clip and started untwisting and retwisting it.

'Well?' he asked.

'We know as much as she does,' Casson replied. Despite his previous resolve to tell Strutt all that Mrs Gordonstoun had told him in confidence, despite his vow to break that confidence unscrupulously, and despite his trust in Strutt, he could not bring himself to do it. The unsolved computation still wove in his head.

'Hmm,' Strutt grunted, squinting at Casson. 'She wouldn't talk, eh?'

'I told her what we knew. She confirmed it. She identified the man.'

'What name did he use?'

'She wouldn't talk,' Casson replied.

Strutt stared at him. Then he looked away.

'Blast them,' he said viciously. 'They never talk. They think of their own precious skins. They never think of the poor mug who's going to be squeezed tomorrow and'll probably blow his ruddy brains out, the silly ass. They never think of the poor blasted copper sweating blood to keep them safe while they sit at home and damn well shiver. Burn them!' He relapsed into silence.

'What now?' Casson asked.

'Well what? You've done all the thinking so far, Mr Sherlock. You tell me.'

Casson reached for his hat, got up, and walked to the door.

'I'll come in some other time,' he said quietly.

There was a crash as the metal ashtray on Strutt's desk clattered on the opposite wall.

'Forget it, Cass,' said Strutt. 'I'm browned off. I'm vexed. I'm irritated. I'm homicidal. I want to beat that little runt's head until he whimpers. Sit down.'

'Fine,' said Casson. 'But take it easy, old cock. Let's be serious about this. What do we do?'

'You understand, Casson, that I'll have to put up this case for full investigation. That means for a prosecution – if we can get one?'

'You can't. Not on present evidence. There isn't any. None of the victims will talk.'

92

'Subpoena them. Make them talk.'

'They'll deny everything.'

'They won't dare.'

'They won't dare to talk. If they deny being blackmailed, they won't be pestered. If they confess it, then trouble – unknown trouble – opens out before them: depositions, appearances in Court, possible exposure by the gossip grapevine. Both friends and enemies will say there's no smoke without fire. They won't dare to talk.'

'Yellow-bellied . . .' Strutt began.

'I'm not so worried about Lockyer and Mrs Gordonstoun,' Casson continued. 'They've bought their trouble. But I am worried about the future victims. We must give them a chance. We must stop Perry from re-becoming Bagot or Martin.'

'Arrest him.'

'You can't. You couldn't hold him. You know that.'

'What do you want me to do? Hire a charabanc and run him over?'

'Frighten him off. Let him know that we are after him, that we'll get him in the end if he goes on playing his pretty little tricks. Make him retire.'

Strutt made a noise like a laugh. It was without humour.

'No criminal retires,' he observed. 'Be your age, Casson. Warn him off and one fine day he'll disappear and go somewhere else and start again. No. I shall put up the case.'

'Perry will get ten years of free living in gaol and his victims – if you get them to talk – will get twenty years of misery each. Is it fair?'

'I'm a copper, not a ruddy author. I deal with facts, not fancies. I'm paid to catch criminals, not to ask if they're kind to spaniels. If somebody else gets hurt in the process and it's not my fault, it's too ruddy bad and I don't give a damn. That's what's known as Law and Order, son. See?'

'All right. I agree. But, if I didn't think that you would catch up with me, I'd shoot the little man myself and then have a good breakfast.'

'So would I,' said Strutt.

'What'll you do then?'

'Leave him alone. More or less alone. For a week or two. Then watch him sporadically.'

'There's another factor,' said Casson. 'Perry's own watching is done in two stages. I learnt that from Mrs Gordonstoun. He must have watched her house until late one night and from dawn the next morning. . . .'

'. . . so she did talk?' Strutt interrupted.

'Not enough,' said Casson and went on: 'Now, when I followed Perry he was never in the Square later than six. Therefore he must have watched her for the first time some weeks or months ago.'

'I think what he does is this. First: he watches his victim to establish a time and a place when the alleged crime took place. He lets his imagined event – imagined at a real time and real place – fester in his mind for some weeks . . .'

'. . . fester is the word . . .'

'. . . until, to him, it has become real, actual, utterly convincing. Second: he watches his victim's house to see what the staff is like, to see the best time to strike, to measure up any possible pitfalls. That was what I saw him doing in Montpelier Square.'

'Probable,' Strutt commented. 'But, if we follow him in the second stage, all we would know is the street he had picked. We wouldn't be able to guess the house or the victim. Or at least we could guess. We couldn't be sure. And we daren't follow him all the time until stage one turns up. It might be for months – he might already have picked his victim and be biding time for stage two – and he would be bound to suspect. So I'll have him followed, once or twice a week, just to check up when he starts his next stage two. There's nothing else we can do.'

'You can do more than guess at the victim. So far they have all banked at Gamman's. If you know the street you can find out which of the residents banks there. The one that does is the victim.'

'Probably,' said Strutt. 'Not certainly. It would still be tricky.'

'We ought to have done that with Montpelier Square. Fool that I was.'

'Anyway, we've got to wait for stage two. Meantime I'll turn the heat on Macfarlane.'

94

Casson had moved over to the window and was looking down Savile Row, fingering his tie, brooding.

'What do you think you'll get there?'

'I have no idea,' Strutt replied. 'But he's new ground. What about you?' he added. 'There's not much you can do now. You've done the hell of a lot. Why don't you pack it up?'

'Macfarlane is your unknown quantity,' said Casson slowly. 'Perry is still mine. I want to know why he does it. I want to know what makes him tick. I want to know if he is savage, or ambitious, or ruthless. I must know *why*. . . .'

'So?'

'I'm going back to Chiswick. I'm going to get into Perry's mind. I'm going to pull it to pieces: slowly, carefully, completely.'

Strutt made no comment until they had shaken hands and were parting in the corridor outside the office. Then all he said was:

'Wash your hands afterwards, won't you? He's diseased.'

Chapter Nine

CASSON mounted his attack in the Shepley Arms. He appeared before Perry's usual time of arrival and stayed at the bar, talking to Peter, while Perry drank his pint and went home. All he did was to stare twice at the blackmailer in such a way that Perry would notice. Once he lifted his tankard as if to go over to him, but put it down again.

The next night he pretended no hesitation. As soon as Perry was settled and had taken his first mouthful of beer, Casson walked over to him and sat down.

'I hope you won't mind my butting in,' he said, 'but I'm sure I've seen you before.' Perry stiffened and seemed about to move away, but Casson went on cheerfully, 'I thought so last night, but I couldn't remember where. I remembered after you had gone. It was Christie's, wasn't it? I often go there, you know.'

Perry seemed to relax a trifle.

'I have been to Christie's,' he replied. It was a prim voice, prim and punctilious, affected in some undefinable way. The affectation was, perhaps, an attempt to cover up the unmistakable trace of an accent.

'So you're a fellow enthusiast,' said Casson. 'That's splendid. It's always exciting to meet another civilized being in the middle of a desert of barbarism' – he waved his arm to indicate the saloon bar. 'The civilized are rare,' he rattled on, praying that Perry was as vain as he calculated he would be, 'and the barbarians are many. Look around you and what do you see? A lot of shoddy stuff used by a lot of stupid people. No sense of beauty among them, no rare perception, no exquisite sense of delicacy. It's gone. It went out with the Regency. And do you know what?' he asked, leaning forward and tapping the table rim emphatically. 'I consider it the duty of people like us to keep those things alive. In fact we're responsible for civilization. We maintain the vision without which a civilization perishes. Don't you agree?'

Perry blinked once, very quickly, like a frog.

'I do,' he said. His eyes were brown.

'My line's pictures,' Casson continued. 'I don't buy for myself, you know. I wish I did, but I can't afford it. However, I've got a number of rich friends and I buy for them when I can pick up a bargain: not that it's often, but the profit's good when it happens. Porcelain too: Rockingham and Chelsea.'

'You are a dealer?' Perry asked in his flat voice, making the words sound more like a statement than a question.

'Lord, no,' Casson laughed. 'I'm a writer. I'm just doing a book about the architecture of Chiswick. I take my own photographs. I must show you sometime. You could probably help me.' Perry seemed alarmed by this oblique offer of collaboration. He made a few politely undistinguished comments, drank up his beer, and left. As the door shut behind him Casson looked at his watch. Perry had cut short his drinking time by seven minutes. Good. An effect had been made.

When John Perry got back to his house in Bickersteth Street, he shut and bolted the front door as was his custom and went upstairs. His breathing was a little quicker than usual and he was possessed by an excitement of conquest.

Although it was still light in the street, light and hot and summery, he lit the used candles in silver George II candlesticks which stood on the mantelshelf in the living-room. He changed into soft, shabby carpet slippers and, as he took his walking shoes into the kitchen and placed them neatly behind the door, he glanced at them with irritated contempt. The uppers, though sound, were cracked and wrinkled and their shape looked as cheap and common as in fact the shoes were. He gazed at them and looked forward to the day when he would have three pairs, each hand-made by a Duke Street bootmaker. Clothes of the same standard, too. But the shoes would be the chief thing and he would be known in the discreet circles in which he moved as the man who wore impeccable shoes.

He went back into the living-room and settled into one of the Queen Anne armchairs which stood on either side of the empty fireplace. He sat there quite still, his hands folded in his lap, and let the excitement carry him where he wanted to go.

It was upsetting meeting strangers like the gentleman in the

Shepley Arms that evening. Upsetting and somehow dangerous. Nevertheless it represented a success. The gentleman had been a connoisseur, a man connected with rich patrons of the arts, a man who wrote books and knew about porcelain – a man of the artistic world, in fact – and he had once talked to him, John Perry, as an equal, as one of the – he searched for the word – one of the *cognoscenti* (he admitted the difficulty of pronunciation and resolved to try and make certain of its phonetics in the dictionary at the Public Library).

That gentleman in the public-house belonged to the world in which he coveted a place, his due place, a world in which hand-made shoes would be unobtrusively noticed and their owner correspondingly elevated in status. True, that world was difficult to enter. Perry felt the muscles of his throat contract for a moment as he thought of the danger, the difficulty of meeting people who were initially hostile: the danger of making a slip in speech, the difficulty of making them aware of his true worth.

His mind slipped round the dangers and played warmly with the path to achievement. It was a comfortable and always rewarding speculation, one that was well detailed from constant repetition, one perennially exciting because it led to the summit of all endeavour.

He would be taken one day into an exclusive Club in St James's Street – taken perhaps by the gentleman in the Shepley Arms. (Never before had he seen the means of introduction so clearly outlined and so almost immediately possible.) They would sit round the fireplace in the sitting-room, a group of them, five or six of them, at any rate not more than seven, all impeccably dressed. They would sip sherry while they made brilliant and sarcastic conversation. He himself would take little share in the dialogue, part of which would be about the scandalous actresses and noblemen of the day and part of which would be a searching analysis of modern art. Now and then one of the well-dressed men would turn to him and ask his opinion, bringing him into the conversation for the sake of courtesy. He would answer quietly, politely, keeping a dignified reserve, yet showing that he had firm convictions. Once or twice he would enter the conversation on his own, making a profound observation, capping another's comment with a witty remark. Gradually the other men would turn more to him, interested in him. He would rise to take his leave. They would press him to stay, to take another glass of sherry. But he would be gently firm. He would collect his hat and gloves and walking-stick, stand on the steps of the Club for a moment, then saunter in the sunlight down St James's Street.

A week later he would be invited to dine. He would cancel another invitation in order to accept. And he could visualize so well what had happened in the interval. After he had left the Club there would have been a moment of silence. Then one of the older men would have turned to the man who introduced him and asked the name of his quiet, rather reserved friend. They would discuss him, recalling his comments, pointing out to each other the dignified wit and profundity of them. They would decide to see more of the stranger to their circle.

So he would dine with them. It would be in a private room of the Club. (Did Clubs have private rooms? he wondered. Should he dine in the dining-room with all the other members? No. This would be a special, a select gathering. It would be a private room.)

There would be candles, polished wood, the finest serviettes, tall, elegant glasses on fine lace mats. As he entered, the group would be talking round the fireplace at the far end of the tall room. His host would detach himself from the circle and come over to him, welcoming him. He would be drawn into the group. The conversation would be general and he would only take a polite part in it, not pushing himself forward, quietly confident of his own knowledge.

Then a leisurely dinner. Champagne, red wine, and port. Fillets of sole, roast chicken, trifle, and several sorts of cheese. Or perhaps they would have heard that he was a gourmet and it would be a simpler but smarter dinner: partridge, savoury, and Stilton. During it he would be asked his opinion of the wine. Smilingly, he would disclaim any specialist knowledge, saying that he had never studied the subject. They would press him for his opinion. He would taste the wine, think for a moment, then speak; and they would find that he had an unusually fine natural judgement. Later, when the conversation was flowing freely with the port and sherry, the talk would turn to artistic and critical appreciation, and he would expound his theory that fine critics were born, not made, that the love of beautiful objects was not an art but an inherent refinement of the faculties, an extra sense which gentlemen had and manual workers did not have. They would agree and he would bring the talk round to ancient Rome, displaying agreeably and modestly an unusual knowledge of his subject.

His meditations expanded and became warmer. One day one of the members of that circle would ask his opinion of a piece of furniture. He would give it, correcting, and rightly correcting, an earlier opinion given by an eminent Cambridge scholar. He would become quietly famous for the excellence of his judgement. In the end he would be invited to join that Club in St. James's Street.

He would become a respected, much sought-after, member. He would be invited to country houses. He might even, like his friend in the Shepley Arms, come to be an adviser on matters of fine art to those of the rich members who were collectors. He would be a well-known figure in the art galleries and showrooms and in Bond Street. And always he would be impeccably dressed, clean shirts of fine linen carefully laundered, unobtrusively expensive suits, discreet silk ties with a small pearl tie-pin, and he would wear small ruby cuff-links, given him by a grateful friend whom he had advised. He uncrossed his legs, recrossed them, and settled more comfortably in his high-backed armchair.

Casson too was speculating. He was sitting by his window on the other side of Bickersteth Street, watching the dull candle-glow from Perry's room, trying to imagine the inside of the black-mailer's thoughts. There seemed to be a discernible pattern in Perry's accusations against his victims: in each case he had imputed to them some sexual irregularity. It might be, of course, that he found this the easiest and most foolproof type of accusation to level. But it might also point to an important factor in Perry's make-up.

The little man was obviously shy of people. Lockyer had been emphatic that Perry was of no interest to women and had hinted strongly that, in his opinion, Perry had never even known one physically. Casson believed that he was right. There seemed no sexual warmth in Perry; in fact, no warmth at all.

Then what was the purpose of the blackmail? Why the accumulation of money? Simply to create a private museum? That had been his first theory but now he was forced to modify it. It was too simple. There must be another motive and it must be something to do with vanity or sex or greed. That was Strutt's view of the motivation of crime and, to some extent, it was Casson's own.

He busied himself in developing his original thesis. He had imagined that Perry collected antiques in order to build an ivory tower, a silent world of valuable possessions which needed no intrusion of embarrassing people. But now his thesis went a stage further. He took Perry's interest in Roman sculpture as a starting point for the new development. Perry admired the Romans. He would admire their cold selfishness, their humourless restraint. He might, therefore, admire the classical type of Roman matron – or his somewhat distorted picture of her. To him she would be a stern and dignified manageress of the household: yet, at the same time, this proud woman would be totally subservient to her husband, bolstering up his ego on the subjection of her own strong personality, making him twice the size he was. Her subservience would appeal to his male vanity, his lack of sexual achievement, while her strength would sooth his mother-complex – if he had one. She would be a slave and protectress at one and the same time; a possession, a mother, and a cook.

There was, however, an alternative theory. Perry might be a homosexual. Casson, being normally sexed and greatly enjoying the company of women, could offer little judgement on this point. But it was possible. Did Perry, then, look to the day when he would install in his private museum some beautiful boy, Pygmalion inside out, a living thing turned into a statue? Surely, if that were so, he would lean towards the Greeks rather than the Romans?

Casson realized that he was making Perry's admiration of Lockyer's Roman bust the pivot for his creation of Perry's character. But it might have been nothing more than an isolated incident, and until he got inside Perry's house and saw what was in the rest of the collection – if there were a collection – he could be no wiser.

At that moment Perry had reached the apotheosis of his dream and his mind was attaching itself idly to fragments of imagination. In one of them he saw himself sitting before luncheon in the window of his Club, watching the elegant women passing down St James's Street. It was more in amused derision than in contempt that he would regard them, those unstable and demanding creatures whose smart clothes brought them only one step away from the jungle. Mentally he sipped his sherry and regarded them. They were not even civilized in their selfishness: and undoubtedly selfishness was a virtue of civilization. They were intermittently selfish, paying an unduly high price to get what they wanted and then throwing away all that they had won as soon as they had won it. There was no stillness in them, nor repose, except that of satiation. They made fools of men and they were fools themselves. If it were not for disciplined people like himself, uncontaminated, aloof, and cultured, civilization would founder in a swamp of expensive and revolting sensuality.

He got up, licked his thumb and forefinger, and snuffed the candle-flames. He went into the back room on the first floor and got his supper, eating it at the plain wood table by the window. It was a simple meal of pilchards, onions, bread and cheese, and a glass of milk. While eating, he read a chapter of Walter Pater's *Renaissance*. Before the daylight broke down completely and made it necessary to switch on the electric light, he prepared for bed in his room on the second floor. When he was undressed, and before he went to bed, he knelt, removed a loose skirting-board, and felt behind to make sure that the tin box in which he kept his pound notes was safe and untouched. Then he got into the old, brass-knobbed bedstead and lay down, flat on his back, his hands clasped across his chest.

The next evening Casson was in the Shepley Arms before Perry got there and, as soon as Perry entered, he acted.

He waved at Perry and insisted on buying him a pint.

'Let's go and sit down,' he said. 'I've got something to show you. They'll interest you.' He sat down and carefully opened the flat paper package which he was carrying.

'They're engravings of scenes in the Peninsular War. Brutal, but wonderfully drawn. The grotesque in art! Look at this. Here you have a peasant being shot by French soldiers while his wife is being raped in the middle of the village street. And here are two dogs playing with each other. What do you think?'

He was watching Perry's eyes, avid to know whether they would dwell longest on the shooting or the rape. But he was disappointed in his search for a clue. Perry glanced at the print without interest and merely said: 'Like animals, aren't they?' and started to drink his beer.

Casson had also brought some of his architectural photographs, and these interested Perry more. Casson led the conversation round to the influence of Greek and Roman originals on English architecture and Perry became almost animated, even confessing his desire to visit Rome, a desire which he might have fulfilled, he said, if only he spoke a foreign language. He recovered himself from this admission of failure by shifting hurriedly to an explanation of his view that specialized knowledge was of no consequence since the connoisseur – by a fraction he mispronounced the word – knew instinctively what was right and what was wrong. He himself never bothered with specialized learning. Casson agreed heartily.

'Furthermore,' said Casson, smiling to himself at his own hypocrisy, 'specialization is actually dangerous. The critical vision may be blurred by considerations of the technique used to make the work of art. You will of course remember what Clive Bell wrote?'

Perry made an inconclusive motion of his head.

'He wrote that fine states of mind – that's to say, exquisitely and fully vivid states of feeling – are the aim of civilized desire. If that's so, then you must be quite ruthless in your pursuit of those fine states. You must rigorously bar out from your consciousness anything which is irrelevant, or disturbing, or unpalatable. You agree?'

Perry not only agreed but leapt upon the theory with some fervour. But, as he launched into his own disquisition, Casson drained his tankard and looked pointedly at its emptiness. Perry hesitated, then rose to his feet.

'I should wish to buy a drink,' he said.

'Thanks. That's decent of you,' Casson replied.

On his way to the bar Perry convinced himself that he had done correctly. This new friend was his gateway to the coveted world of his dreams. He must start some time or all his labours would be wasted. He would buy the gentleman a drink: as any gentleman would do. Could he make do with a half-pint? No. He would have to buy a pint – as the gentleman had bought for him.

He brought two pints back to their table.

'You think that one must really be ruthless in winning those states of mind you were talking about?' he asked eagerly.

Casson parried the question. He wanted to know what Perry felt about ruthlessness.

'Don't you?' he asked in his turn.

'Yes,' Perry answered. He took a sip of his beer and carefully put down his tankard. He seemed emboldened. 'Yes,' he went on in another burst of talk, 'I do think that you are right. A person should be clear-minded about it: what I myself would call skilfully selfish. In other words, a person should do everything he can to suit himself without actually endangering himself. That would be silly and disagreeable.' Equally suddenly the urge to talk dried up in him and he fell silent, gazing into his beer.

Casson told him stories of his rich collector friends, most of them invented, and Perry's interest warmed again. Casson finished his second pint and put down his tankard with a bang on the table.

'Have a chaser with me,' he suggested. 'I always do when I'm dining in town.' Perry shook his head.

'I never touch spirits,' he said. 'No, thank you. I really must be going home.' He glanced at the clock on the wall. 'I'm twenty minutes late. I must be going.'

'One for the road,' Casson insisted. 'Does you all the good in the world. A painter friend of mine always drinks chasers. He says that's the only point in having beer. Have a sherry if you don't like whisky?'

Reluctantly Perry accepted. He regretted the acceptance. Then he said to himself that he must be firm, he must teach himself to live like the upper-class friends he hoped to make. You must start some time, he assured himself.

Casson had a whisky and bought Perry a large Amontillado. Perry tried to sip his very slowly, but Casson forced the pace, and when they left the pub together Perry was walking with deliberation.

'You seem to know a lot about works of art,' said Casson as they moved off up the road. 'Have you done any collecting?'

Resolve took hold of Perry. Hitherto he had only dreamed of a cultured, sophisticated world in which he would display his knowledge, and in which his treasures would display him. Now he must set his foot on the ladder. Now was the moment. There was always a risk in starting but it had to be done. Well, if there was a risk, he would take it. He would be ruthless in choosing his moment.

'I have,' he replied. 'As a matter of fact I have got quite a nice collection. It is small, of course. Would you care to see it?'

'If you're not too busy,' said Casson casually, trying to keep the triumph out of his voice.

Chapter Ten

ON the step Perry fumbled for a moment with his latch-key, then opened the door, let Casson in, shut and bolted the door after him. He switched on the light.

A naked, twenty-five watt bulb illuminated the drab, linoleum-covered staircase. On the walls as they went up the stairs, Casson noticed two engravings, one of Blenheim, one of Castle Howard. They came on to a small landing at the end of the first flight. Perry went ahead into the living-room.

'Wait a minute,' Perry called out. 'I'm going to light up.'

There was the rasp and flare of a match. Casson waited, peering up to the second storey, trying to see the shape of the house above them in the darkness.

The living-room began to glow with the light of candles.

'Come in,' Perry called. Casson went in.

The mantelpiece was such as you would expect to find in any house along that street but on it were two silver Georgian candlesticks. Quite good ones, Casson thought, though he knew little about silver.

The fireplace was framed by two high-backed wing armchairs, upholstered in dull gold brocade with purple piping. Definitely Queen Anne. Against the wall opposite the fireplace was a Sheraton sofa-table. Casson went over to examine it, admired its polish, and wondered if the handles on the twin drawers were original. On the sofa-table stood a set of six Bristol glass goblets of a very cold, very dark, menacing blue. Either side of the table, against the wall, was a mahogany shield-back chair – almost certainly Hepplewhite. It was clear that Perry bought well, though whether it was by luck or good judgement Casson could not yet tell.

Before the window stood a small secretaire, about three and a half feet in height. Casson once, idly acquisitive of knowledge, had learnt something about woods and identified it as being made of harewood, with Ringwood banding. It was the sort of piece at which eighteenth-century gentlemen would have sat, toying with their personal and laboured translations of Catullus into English verse, or checking their wine merchant's account for purchases of Bucellas, Madeira, and Hollands. On the pretence of examining its craftsmanship, Casson opened its writing flap. The pigeon holes were pathetically empty, peopled only by an old quill pen, a bottle of Swan ink, and a laundry book. He shut the flap, and picked up from the top of the secretaire the two bronze statu-ettes: boy with javelin and boy with bow: both launching their static shafts into the silent room. He put them down and turned back into the room. The rug beneath his feet was blue-and-gold in the light of the candles, threaded through with a motif of gleaming purple, and it looked good, very good. Casson wished he knew something about carpets since he dearly wanted to know what it cost. He estimated the value of the antiques in the room at about four hundred pounds: perhaps more if you included the rug. And bought over several years. Which meant that Perry, to pay his rent and daily bills as well, would need about seven hundred a year. More of course, if he were saving up for his ulti-mate retirement from crime.

They chatted for some time, mainly about furniture and the alleged iniquities of antique dealers. Then Perry asked a question which startled Casson.

'I suppose you go a lot to Clubs in London?'

'Oh, yes,' Casson replied, wondering what the devil he was driving at. 'Quite a lot.'

'And I suppose most of the members have furniture like this?' Perry continued, looking round the room. Casson remembered Nigel Willington's untidy house and grinned.

'Some do,' he said. 'The richer ones, of course. But not all of them appreciate these things, you know.'

'I suppose most of them are rich?' Perry asked. Casson thought he saw daylight and his heart hammered. Perry was sounding him out, intending to use him as a pointer who would scent and indicate the rich prey in the Clubs. Surely and cautiously Perry was trapping himself.

'I know quite a number of rich ones,' Casson replied. 'Some are very nice, you know. Some pretty dull. I buy pictures for one or two of them. It's sad really. They just don't know what to do with their money and I doubt if they appreciate the pictures I buy. But it's fun for me, so I don't mind. They're an odd lot, very eccentric in many ways; then again, a few really do know what they're after. They would interest you.'

'Yes. They would.' Perry sat in thought, then appeared to be getting drowsy. Casson rose to his feet and stretched. He did not wish to overplay his hand.

'I really must be off,' he said. 'I've got some more writing to do. Thanks for the interesting evening.'

Perry saw him out and Casson heard the bolt click after him. He strolled across the street, humming. Life was good and life was the chase.

Perry went back upstairs to the living-room. He was in a mulled haze of satisfaction. He moved slowly round the room, touching the cold bronze of the statuettes, touching the white metal of the candlesticks, rubbing his finger-tips lightly over the surface of the sofa-table, holding up to the candlelight the blue Bristol glasses and feeling the weight of them.

His feet were hot. He changed into the bedroom slippers for which they yearned and sat down in an armchair, relaxed, brooding. He had been so right to seize the opportunity, to ask that pleasant Mr Duke to see his collection. Mr Duke was the first man who had seen it. There was a certain danger in his seeing it but the danger had to be risked if he were ever to rise and mix with connoisseurs. Mr Duke knew many of them and he knew the West End Clubs. In time he would introduce Perry and then ... the dream was not so much of a dream after all. It only needed time to make it a reality: time and resolve. That was what made him different from other men – the resolve to translate his dream into reality, the ruthlessness to get what he wanted and what he knew to be his proper station in life.

What might have been a thin, muffled laugh came from him as he sat there. He had remembered a conversation which he had overheard at the Bank one day. Two of his colleagues, athletic, popular men whom he despised, had been discussing him.

'Perry's a funny old stick,' said one. 'Like a mouse with a temper.'

'Temper?' queried the other. 'He couldn't scare a fly.'

'I don't know. I think he could if you goaded him long enough. These quiet blokes do, you know.'

'Don't believe it,' said the other. 'He's just an insignificant little fellow whom you wouldn't recognize again if you met him in the street. And I'll bet you wouldn't either. I say, we've got a new typist coming . . .'

That had been the crucial moment, Perry remembered. He had been hurt, then angry, then – suddenly and coldly – determined. It was as if he had been forced to a decision which had been nagging him for years.

They had done him a service, those gross fools in the bank. He had determined to show himself that he was different from them, more cunning, more able, more of a character. And his determination was directed by their comment on his insignificance. If he could not be recognized twice in the street, then crime would be safe: if it were a safe crime. Blackmail was safe, so long as you tapped your victim once. And blackmail would get him the money to buy the beautiful things for which he yearned; unspeaking, unhostile things whose presence would be a continual praise of his own refinement.

For two years he had spent every moment he could in studying the accounts of his bank's clients, amassing knowledge, knowledge, knowledge. Then he had retired. And they had even given him a fountain pen! Now he was independent, resolute, cultured while they – those black-coated oafs – were still cashiers or clerks.

Mr Duke had been so right. A person must be ruthless to get and ruthless to guard. He owed that to himself. Cultured people were rare and they were important to culture. They must preserve their fine sensibilities. They must be ruthless in self-preservation with a cunning which those fools in the Bank could never dream of.

He was in the same elevated spirit of mind the next morning as he dusted his furniture, dusted and polished, made his bed and washed up the supper things. He even whistled a toneless tune as he changed from his shopping clothes into his black suit with its pin-stripe trousers, making himself ready for his customary sandwich with Macfarlane in the City.

Casson went to the Shepley Arms that evening as usual but Perry did not appear. Casson was disappointed but nothing more. But when Perry failed to turn up at the pub for the next two nights he became alarmed. Had he sprinkled his bait too obviously? Had the shy animal retired to its lair?

On the morning of the fourth day Casson kept watch at his window. Perry went out as usual and returned an hour later with his shopping bag. So he was there all right. But why had he broken his habit of going to the Shepley Arms? Why should he break it unless he were afraid of meeting Casson?

In the end Casson rang Strutt.

'I'm glad you rang up,' said Strutt's voice. 'Something queer is going on.'

'I know,' replied Casson. 'I was getting on well with him and then he sheered off. He hasn't been to the pub for days.'

'No, he hasn't. He's been with Macfarlane.'

'Macfarlane?' Casson was doubly disturbed. This was quite beyond expectation. It was abnormal, out of routine. It was disappointing, too, since it had seemed that Perry was sounding out Casson as a new provider of information and yet he was seeing even more of Macfarlane.

'Are you busy?' Strutt asked.

'No.'

'Come on over and have a drink. I'm at the nick at the moment. I'll meet you in The Guinea in Bruton Place. When?'

'Come into the office instead,' said Casson. 'I'll be there in half an hour, and we'll be more private. I'll tell Tippett you're coming and he'll get some lager for you.'

'Right-ho, son.' Strutt rang off.

When Casson got up to Manton and Heywood, the Superintendent had already arrived and was bulging out of the armchair in the inner office. He started talking as soon as Casson shut the door.

'It's odd,' he said. 'But I think it's good. The boys have been on to Macfarlane. He's pretty easy – regular hours of work, coffee at ten forty five, lunch at twelve. Four days ago they took him to a sandwich bar in the City – the one you told us about – '

'"John's"?'

'The same. He and Perry had a sandwich. We couldn't hear what they were nattering about. Young Macfarlane says something and laughs. Pokes Perry in the ribs with his finger. Sort of a joke, it looks like. Perry goes as white as a blasted sheet. Practically starts shaking. Most unusual. He calms down a bit and they finish their lunch and Mac goes back to the bank. Does Perry go home? Not on your ruddy life. He prowls about like a hungry dog. Mac won't leave the bank till five-thirty so my lad goes after Perry. He sits in Hyde Park till four and then he goes off, looking sick as mud.' Strutt took a pull of lager.

'Next evening they meet again. In a pub. This time it's Mac's turn to go white. Then he goes red, then white again. Like a set of blasted traffic lights. Then he gets angry. Perry calms him down. It looks as if he's arguing, persuading, but we can't get near enough to hear. They have a couple of drinks and go out. The last thing Mac says to Perry is, "I won't believe it. I can't." "It's true," says Perry, "but you'll never get the truth, Jim. You can't trust what a woman says. Not under those circumstances. You know you can't." He sounds sad, sad and wise, the crawling bastard.

'Yesterday evening Mac goes out to Putney and collects his fiancée. . . .'

'Fiancée?'

'Girl named Jean Shaw. Disraeli Road, Putney. She lodges there. They go out for a walk on the Heath. They have a row, poor souls. A real blazer, it looks. She walks off with her head in the air, trying not to cry. I suppose she goes home. We don't know because our man is still on Macfarlane. Mac goes back to his flat in Shaftesbury Avenue. We keep an eye on the joint. After half an hour in goes Perry. Three quarters of an hour out they come, Mr Perry looking as pleased as Mr Blasted Punch. They go to a pub. The argument goes on. Macfarlane looks pretty ropy. He drinks gin, too much gin, but he gets home all right. There you are.'

'They've quarrelled?'

'Yes.'

'About what?'

'The loot. Crooks always do.'

'I think it's the girl. Perry's afraid of her. He thinks Macfarlane might split to her. He thinks she might go to the police.'

'She wouldn't go to the police if her boy-friend's mixed up in blackmail,' Strutt observed wryly.

'Then he thinks she might stop the boy playing along with him. By every count he must get Macfarlane away from the girl. Unless she's an accomplice already?'

'I think not.' Strutt finished his lager and poured more. Watching him made Casson thirsty. He rang for Tippett and asked him to fetch up a bottle of Moselle from the cellar.

'It's all good,' said Strutt. 'Whatever happens young Mac is in a spot. If he goes on with Perry he'll have to risk the girl finding out and breaking off the engagement. If he tries to cut loose from Perry, Perry'll shop him. Perry's probably got something on Mac, some petty misdemeanour, something to bind him. Either way Mac's for it and believe you me he's looking as ropy as hell.'

'So?'

'We let the strain work on him till he's cracking. Then we get him. He'll squeal. I think I'll put a man on to Perry as well. In the daytime, anyway.' He made a note on an old envelope.

'What's the girl's address?' Casson asked.

Strutt gave it to him.

'You can't be certain that she hasn't been told by Macfarlane,' said Casson. 'If she does know anything, she may break first. We could promise to get her boy friend off lightly. Queen's evidence and all that.'

'You're not going to try your deadly charm on her?'

Casson grinned.

'I'll put Mrs Baker on the job, my housekeeper. She's a friendly old dear and as cunning as you wouldn't suspect. Has Macfarlane got a char?'

'Yes.'

'Give me her address too. Mrs Baker can do her as well. We may get something there. Does Macfarlane normally drink?'

'Don't know. Too early to say.'

'I'll find out.'

Strutt finished his lager, accepted one of Casson's cigars, and left. Casson went back to Mount Street to instruct Mrs Baker.

Her reports were tantalizing. The young man and the girl continued to quarrel. A nice, quiet girl, commented Mrs Baker, Lowland Scots and a decent sort. Would make any mother-in-law
happy. Wished she'd had a daughter-in-law like that herself.
Macfarlane saw Perry almost every evening, always in a pub. He
drank more than Perry and he drank more than was good for him.
From his char, a voluble and licentious soul who lived in Lamb's
Conduit Street, Mrs Baker learnt that her young man never had a
drop of drink in the house and, as far as she knew, never drank
anyway. Keen on physical fitness, he was, said the char. Not
the heavy-drinking sort, she had added with a profundity of
wisdom.

For Casson and Strutt the strain grew. Obviously the moment
was approaching ripeness but Strutt counselled delay. Let the
plum drop, he urged. Casson was compelled to agree.

The reports on Perry produced only one new factor. He went
to Brighton for the day. He took a room in the same hotel. He
stayed in his room the whole time. He travelled back to London
in the evening. It was identical with the outing which he had made
before he blackmailed Mrs Gordonstoun.

Casson and Strutt talked it over.

'He must do it for a reason,' Casson argued.

'Probably needed a break.'

'He does nothing without a reason.'

'Then he's thinking up a new victim. I don't know. We'll have
to wait and see. I'm much more interested in Macfarlane right
now. If he cracks, we've got Perry. Let's sit tight.'

But Casson fretted. There was something that did not fit, some
false quantity in their calculations. Evening after evening he puzzled but could get no answer. One night he even drank himself
into a stupor to see if a sudden shaft of illumination would well
up in his brain. But there was no *in vino veritas* and the only result
was a fierce hangover.

His mind needled him remorselessly. Surely Perry would not
take the risk of Macfarlane breaking the wrong way? Surely he
would reckon that he might be driving Macfarlane to confess to
the girl? But, whichever way he argued it, he had to return to
Strutt's conclusion. Sit tight and wait.

Later that week Mrs Baker returned to Mount Street at a quarter to one, smelling strongly of port but completely sober.

'Had a regular do, they did, sir,' she related. 'Thought I'd better come and tell you. The two gentlemen sat in the saloon bar from seven till half past ten and had to see each other home. That's to say Mr Perry saw the young gentleman home because he wasn't so squiffy, sir. He stays in the young gentleman's flat till a bit before midnight. He comes out and shuts the door. Least, he starts to. He fumbles in his sleeve. . . .'

'In his sleeve?'

'In both sleeves. He looks fussed. He hunts in his pockets. He brings a handkerchief out of his trousers pocket, looks at it for a moment, and tucks it up his sleeve. He shuts the door. He goes off to the tube at Piccadilly. Sober as a judge he was then. Least, that's how he looked.'

It seemed as though Macfarlane was breaking at last.

Casson tossed in bed, listening to the wind playing with itself in the Farm Street Gardens. Why was Perry fussed about his handkerchief? He obviously did not want to blow his nose and, if he had left it in the flat he could have got it back from Macfarlane the next day. Unless there was some reason why it shouldn't be left there. What reason? Something had happened.

He woke early and was out of the flat before breakfast. He was heavy with doubt, certain that somehow he and Strutt had miscalculated. He walked quickly to Shaftesbury Avenue, found the block in which Macfarlane lived, and went in.

He stopped on the fourth floor. There was a smell of gas. He sniffed and raced up the last flight. The smell got stronger. He found the door and hammered on it. There was no reply. He bent down to sniff at the keyhole and recoiled. He hammered on the door again, then turned to run down the stairs and fetch the porter.

He got down two flights when he met a stout, red-cheeked woman puffing her way up.

'Are you Mr Macfarlane's ch— do you do for him?' he demanded.

'Yes.' The word came between gasps for breath. 'Fair kill me these stairs do,' she added, coughing.

'Give me the key,' he said. 'Something's happened.'

'That's all right, luv,' she puffed, going on up the stairs. 'Time'll tell, as I always say.' She mounted slowly, and Casson could have kicked her. Outside the door she fumbled for the key in her bag.

'Now that's the key of me house,' she said. 'And this is the key of the shed where me old man keeps his motor bicycle.' Casson's fury increased. She turned her bag the other way and groped again. 'Ah, here it is. In the lining.' Casson grabbed it and at last the door opened. He choked.

'Stay in the hall,' he shouted behind him, groping his way into a dark room beyond it. 'Switch on the light.' The lights came up in the room. He saw a door ahead of him. He wrenched the handle, opened it and rushed in. He tripped and fell with a crash against the bed, coughing with the cloying intensity of the smell. He tottered back into the other room, took a deep breath, and went back into the bedroom, feeling his way to the window. He found it, ripped back the flimsy curtains, and flung up the bottom sash. Daylight and fresh air flooded it.

He took one look at the crumpled bed and a second at the fireplace. But the char had followed him coughing continuously, and was lumbering towards the gas fire.

'Don't touch it!' Casson yelled. He pulled his handkerchief out of his pocket, wound it round his hand, gripped the gas-tap by its edges, and turned it off.

'Out of here! Quick!' he ordered the charwoman.

He turned towards the bed. There was Macfarlane, fully dressed, his tie pulled down from his throat, tousled, unshaven, rumpled.

Casson bent over him and felt for his heart. He straightened up again and walked carefully back to the door. Jim Macfarlane was not only tousled; he was also dead.

Chapter Eleven

THE char was gazing at the sprawled heap on the bed.

'What's happened to him, sir?' she gasped.

Casson took her by the shoulders and swivelled her round towards the bedroom door. But her body was too heavy for her feet. She started to topple and he had to hold her up. He propelled her gently out of the bedroom, through the small sitting-room and out into the hall.

'There's been an accident,' he said. 'Go downstairs and fetch the porter. I suppose there is a porter?'

'Oh yes. Mr O'Connor.' She sniffed, then started coughing.

'Well, you fetch him,' said Casson. He hoped that the long trek down, the consequent argument, and the even more arduous climb back up the stairs would keep her away for some time. He locked the door behind her and went back through the flat.

He bent over the bed and carefully turned the humped body so that it lay on its front. He tried to give it artificial respiration, his eyes shut and his own breath coming bitterly against the reek of gas in the room, praying that by some miracle life might jump and move in the sluggish, unwieldly limbs. In the end, choking, he had to stop. He groped his way into the sitting-room and sat down, his head bowed between his knees, searching for breath. Then he went back to the bedroom and began all over again. Once hope flared as he thought he saw the muscles of Macfarlane's mouth twitch and contract; but the hope died as quickly as it had come and he had to accept what he had known before – that it was too late. He gave up, horrified at the picture which he must have presented, sitting astride an inert body, pumping at its lungs, struggling with it to get it to gulp, to take and accept the life-giving air. They must have looked like two gruesome acrobats, a live man and a corpse grappling in the futile attempt to evoke existence.

Tenderly he laid the body back as it originally was, careful not to touch the medicine bottle lying on the bed. He looked round the room to note all the details and impress them on his memory, and went through into the sitting-room.

He wrapped his hand once again in his handkerchief, lifted the telephone receiver off its cradle, and dialled Strutt's number in Fulham.

Adeline answered, her voice happy and warm and living.

'Cass!' she said. 'How nice. I thought you never got up before ten. . . .'

'It's trouble,' he said. Her voice changed.

'I see. I'll fetch George.'

Casson waited for nearly half a minute, listening to the shuffling and whispering outside the locked door of Macfarlane's flat.

'What is it?' Strutt asked.

'Macfarlane. Dead.'

'Dead? How? How do you know?'

'Gas.'

'Gassed himself? Damn.'

'No.'

'Don't speak in riddles. What's happened?'

'Macfarlane is dead,' said Casson slowly and distinctly. 'He did not commit suicide. He was murdered.'

There was a pause at the other end of the line. When Strutt spoke again his voice was coldly matter-of-fact.

'Where are you?'

'In Macfarlane's flat.'

'You're sure he's dead?'

'Yes.'

'Tried to make him sick?'

'I have given him artificial respiration. He won't take it. He's as dead as he ever will be.'

'All right. I'll ring the nick and get a doctor along. I'll be with you. Don't let anyone in till I come.'

' You may need the fingerprint boys. . . .'

'Don't waste my time,' said Strutt and rang off.

There was a tapping on the front door of the flat. Casson ignored it and returned to the bedroom. His toe caught in the mat over which he had tripped when he first rushed in. He lifted his foot to kick it away but changed his mind and bent to examine it. It showed nothing.

He looked round the room, at the photograph of a girl on the wardrobe, at the two cheap hairbrushes, the enamel cuff-links and the scattered loose change on the narrow mantelpiece, at the tweed suit hanging behind the door and the small pile of paper-backed books on the bedside table. His gaze fixed itself on the tooth-mug by the books. It still held some liquid.

He looked at the body. He had seen death in battle, but then it had been merely a hurried detail in a noisy action. This was different. He could imagine that the vacant body of Macfarlane was still being watched by the same sly premeditation that had killed it. Casson was repelled: fascinated and repelled. The cherry-red of the corpse's lips mocked and sickened him.

He went through and unlocked the door of the flat. The charwoman was half-turned away from him, holding on to the iron railing of the stairway, talking to a sturdy, bullet-headed man with a red face and large ears. He wore a waistcoat but no jacket.

''Oo are you?' he demanded as Casson came out.

Casson eyed him with some distaste. Slowly he took out his gold cigarette case, selected a cigarette and lit it. Then, once more he contemplated the truculent, red-faced man before him.

'What is your name?' he asked gently.

'I'll 'ave none o' that. I find you in one of me client's flats, and I want to know 'oo the 'ell you are and wot the 'ell you're doing there.'

'What is your name?' Casson asked coldly.

The other hesitated.

'O'Connor.' Casson waited for the word 'Sir' but it stuck in the man's throat. 'I'm the porter 'ere. But what I want to know is . . .'

'There's been an accident.'

The charwoman lumbered forward. 'What is it, sir?' She tried to push past Casson but O'Connor seized her arm.

'Now then, Mrs Queenleigh,' he said sharply. 'Don't you go rushing in. There's something fishy going on 'ere.' He turned to Casson. 'Now then, you, what's up?' He tried to put on a show of authority.

Casson paid no attention to him.

'You are Mrs Queenleigh?' he asked her.

'Yes, sir. Violet. Violet Queenleigh. Me husband's a butcher. Best in Clerkenwell, I'd say. Has there been an accident?'

'There has.'

'I knew it . . .' she began.

'Knew what?' he asked sharply.

'That something would happen. It said so in me Stars. You must meet trouble as it comes, it said, and I knew something would happen, though me husband laughs at them.'

Their colloquy had attracted a small and dispirited audience. A listless man of uncertain age and with heavily pouched eyes had shuffled up the stone stairs. He wore baggy, frayed tweeds and a bow tie. One of his shirt-buttons was undone. He stood silently, one hand on the pocket of his coat, his eyes shifting furtively from one to the other of the three people in front of him. As Mrs Queenleigh was being cut short by O'Connor in the middle of her aphorisms on the meaning of the Stars a door opened from the flat on the other side of the landing and a woman came out. She had the hard, strained look of a woman of fifty-eight who is trying to keep the attractiveness which she once possessed. Her carefully made-up Cupid's bow mouth seemed pitifully lecherous in the polished morning light. She looked with a quick, hostile stare at the group and went back into her flat, turning for a last glance at Casson before she shut the door.

Casson sighed with depression. Macfarlane had gone to Hades or Nirvana, or wherever the dead did go, he had been obliterated or sent on the most important exploration of his life, he had been forced into the discovery of death; and all that he, Casson, could notice were an undone shirt-button and a useless scarlet mouth.

He nodded towards Mrs Queenleigh and said to the porter:

'Take her downstairs and look after her.'

'I want to know 'oo the 'ell you think you . . .'

'Take her downstairs,' snapped Casson. O'Connor looked nasty, then began to obey.

He was forestalled by Strutt. The Superintendent came shambling up the stairs at a remarkable pace for a man of his build, moving sideways like a crab.

'I'm a Police Officer,' he said to the porter. 'Who are you?'

O'Connor eyed him without pleasure.

'Michael O'Connor,' he said.

'And you?' said Strutt to the charwoman.

'Violet Queenleigh, sir. This gentleman says there's been a dreadful accid—'

'And you?' Strutt snapped to the listless man with the pouched eyes.

'I'm – er – that is to say I – er – live here and – er . . .'

'What's your name?'

'Irwin Standing. I am . . .'

Strutt squinted at him and gave him a cold grin.

'Well, stop standing about here.' He turned to the porter.

'I'll want you later. And this woman.' He swivelled to Casson. 'Now.'

Casson unlocked the door and Strutt charged in, his head lowered as though he were meeting an invisible force.

'Shut the door,' he said over his shoulder. He went straight through into the bedroom. The smell of gas still sickened the air.

The squat policeman bent over the body for a moment, but peered for a longer time at the medicine bottle which lay on the rucked blanket. He sniffed the tooth-mug, glanced at the scattered objects on the mantelpiece and the wardrobe, inspected the window. He came back to the bedroom door.

'The mat?' he queried.

'Yes,' Casson replied. 'It was up against the door. I tripped over it when I came in.'

Strutt grunted.

'Looks like suicide. Clear as a ruddy bell.'

'It wasn't suicide.'

Strutt grunted again and stood motionless in the middle of the room, his arms hanging by his side, his gaze fixed on the bedclothes. Casson took out a cigarette and was about to light it.

'Not in here,' said Strutt, never looking at him. 'We'll want to see if there's any other ash. Macfarlane didn't smoke.' Casson put it away.

'Why not suicide?' Strutt asked, still motionless.

'I'm sure it wasn't.' He told him about Perry and the handkerchief.

'You think it was fixed?'

'By John Perry.'

'Why did you come here this morning?'

Casson was pursuing another line of thought.

'You will have noticed that Mrs Queenleigh is a first-rate cleaner. You've only got to look at the brass fender next door. The odds are that she cleaned the tap of the gas-fire. It certainly looks like it. If she did, there will be no fingerprints on it even though it was turned on. Perry had to turn it on himself, and he didn't dare leave prints. Now, no suicide puts on gloves before he gasses himself: nor does he wipe the tap after he's turned it on.'

'I dunno,' Strutt observed, not looking up. 'Suicides do odd things. We had a chap who threw himself out of a window in Davies Street. The silly ass landed on top of a taxi and only broke his ankle. But he had filled up his fountain pen before he jumped, and the only thing he worried about in hospital was whether the ruddy thing had leaked.'

'Macfarlane wouldn't have wiped the tap. He was drunk . . .'

'Was he?'

'Mrs Baker followed him and Perry.'

'I'll get my report when I go to the nick.'

'If you find no prints on that tap, it was murder,' Casson concluded.

'Maybe.' They moved into the sitting-room.

Then the procession started. The police doctor, a tired, taut man came, had a whispered conversation with Strutt, spent some time in the bedroom, and left. Two police photographers moved in with tripods, cameras, and flashlamps. Casson watched them in action. They were unconversationally efficient and clearly regarded the body on the bed as a mere object to be recorded. The fingerprint expert listened to Strutt's instructions, nodded and got down to work. Casson wandered back to the sitting-room.

Strutt came in, holding the bedroom doormat. He did not look at Casson.

'I should shove off, Cass,' he said. 'There's nothing you can do here. I'll need you this evening. I'm afraid you'll have to make a statement.'

'I'll be at the office till lunch-time. Then I'll go back to Mount Street. You can ring me there.'

Strutt did not answer. Casson let himself out of the flat, brushed through the untidy group of people who were hanging about on the stairs and walked as quickly as he could to Vigo Street, hoping to shake off the scent of gas.

He tried to keep his mind away from Macfarlane by concentrating on his correspondence from the vineyards of Epernay and the Médoc and by planning a trip through the Gironde and Cognac during the time of the coming autumn vintage. But the names had lost all their usual, ringing magic. Cantenac, Margaux, even Smith-Haut-Lafitte, had become empty arrangements of vowels and consonants, devoid of sunlight, earth, and the noise of farmhouse kitchens.

He went back to his flat. Walking up through Berkeley Square he felt detached, as though he had been drinking wine on an empty stomach, for Macfarlane was a reality greater than the parked motor-cars and the cockaded porter outside the Connaught Hotel.

Mrs Baker made him an omelette, but he could not finish it; nor could he face the salad of sliced tomato and onion. He opened a bottle of Burgundy, feeling that he needed its heavy magnificence to permeate and soothe his mind. He put the full glass in the sunlight on the window table and, while it gently warmed, he watched the truncated purple globe. The noise of screaming, playing children in the Gardens below faded as they went back into school.

He picked up the glass and drank a mouthful. The wine was deep and rich and immensely vital. It was an animal which one drank. Perhaps that was why the Homeric Greeks offered wine to their gods and their dead.

He tipped the glass slightly so that the wine slipped over its far rim and fell, drop by drop, on the carpet. A libation to the dead! An appeasement to the invisible, inevitable gods who now had young Jim Macfarlane in their remote embrace! Drop after drop the libation spattered on the carpet.

Suddenly he realized what he was doing. He straightened up. He was interested to find that he was shivering.

Strutt did not telephone until eight o'clock that evening. When he did, Casson went down to the Savile Row Police Station. Strutt was sitting in his office, coatless, his desk covered with foolscap sheets of handwritten paper. A half-empty teacup and a plate with biscuit crumbs stood on top of the pile of telephone directories on the window-sill.

'Well?' Casson asked. Strutt did not look up.

'He was gassed all right. That's how he died. But he took a stiff dose of sleeping draught. . . .'

'Sleeping draught? Macfarlane?'

'Yes.'

'But he wouldn't need anything to make him sleep. He was a healthy young man; the sort of fellow who'd go to sleep as soon as he got into bed, then get up at half past six in the morning and go for a run.'

'Well, he did. It was in the tooth-glass,' said Strutt. 'He got the prescription from a doctor he went to at the beginning of last week. We traced the chemist . . .'

'. . . from the medicine bottle on the bed?'

'And we've got the prescription. We're checking with the doctor. I want to know what reason Macfarlane gave for needing dope.'

'What was it?'

'Chloral hydrate. The Mickey Finn. It can be lethal.'

'You don't think he took, or was given, an overdose?'

'Hard to tell. The croaker is checking at the post-mortem. But I calculate the medicine bottle only held enough for seven or eight doses. If Macfarlane had been taking it regularly, there would only have been enough left for an ordinary dose. And he hadn't got any more of the stuff. We searched the flat.'

'Was the girl on his mind?'

'I don't know. We picked her up as she left her office – solicitors in Essex Street – and brought her along here. She's a good girl. She went the colour of whitewash but her voice never faltered. She said they'd had a quarrel or two because he'd been pressing her to marry him as soon as possible and she didn't want to be rushed into it. She said he'd seemed nervous and irritable over the last week or two. That's all. I think she's hiding something.' He picked a paper-clip out of the tin tray on his desk and started to unwind it. 'Ruddy nuisance these loyal girls,' he observed.

'Do you think she knows about Perry?'

Strutt grimaced and threw the unwound clip into the wastepaper basket.

'I don't think so. But you can never tell how nice a nice girl is until you can prove it. She might be a little vixen. She might be hiding a lot. I don't know. As a matter of fact I don't think I know anything at all about women. You'd better have a go at her. You seem to know a lot about them.' He squinted at Casson and took up another paper-clip. Casson did not reply to the invitation.

'Were there any fingerprints on the gas-tap?' he asked.

'Not one. Clean as a baby's bottom.'

'So Macfarlane couldn't have turned it on?'

Strutt shrugged.

'Probably not. It's not proof. There's not a tag of evidence that Macfarlane was murdered. Even that damned doormat goes to prove that he committed suicide. . . .'

'. . . you know how it was done?'

'Pulled up against the door from outside by cotton or something and the cotton pulled away afterwards.'

'It's perfectly possible. I tried it in my flat this afternoon. Mrs Baker thought I was mad.'

'The Coroner would think I was barmy too if I started producing theories like that in Court,' Strutt remarked. 'You know perfectly well that everything points to suicide: the quarrels, the sleeping draught, the sudden drinking and getting plastered – everything.'

'Except Macfarlane's character. He wouldn't ever take his own life. It's psychologically impossible.'

'Tell that to the Coroner.'

'Don't you think so?' Casson persisted.

Strutt picked up the telephone.

'I must ring this boy's parents,' he said. 'We've formally identified the corpse but they may want to come down and see it. And then there's the inquest. They live in Lockerbie, wherever the hell that is,' he added.

'Dumfriesshire,' said Casson. 'I know it well. I used to shoot pheasants up that way at one time.'

'I expect they were proud of him,' said Strutt. 'Poor devils. His dad's a farmer. You can imagine him: hard-working, God-fearing – only the Lowland Scots know how to fear God. A decent, honest, respectable man: unlike us,' he added, bitterly. 'I wish to goodness I wasn't a blasted copper.'

When the call came through and was over, Strutt got up from his desk and slouched over to the window. He stood there for some moments, looking down into the street. Without turning round he said:

'I agree with you, Cass. Macfarlane was murdered. He was murdered by Perry. That's why Perry went to Brighton. To prepare himself. But we can't prove it.' There was silence between them.

'There's nothing to go on? Nothing at all?' Casson asked in the end.

'Nothing. Except for the chloral bottle. There were a number of smudged prints on it. And some clear ones. But they were all placed in such a way that the person holding the bottle must have held it upside down and all the chloral would have run out. Unless it was empty when he held it.'

'Whose were the prints?'

'Macfarlane's, of course. Whose did you expect?'

'He was drunk.'

'You don't hold a bottle neck downwards: not even if you are drunk. You can't undo it.'

'Yes?'

'So Perry poured the dose for the plastered Macfarlane. He used gloves or wrapped his hand in the handkerchief or something. When Macfarlane was doped, Perry gripped his hand round the bottle so that there were certain to be some clear prints of Macfarlane's. That was necessary to the alibi. But he must have had a moment of panic or been thinking about something else because he fastened the fingers on the medicine bottle in the wrong way. Even so, it's not proof. It's scarcely evidence.'

'You don't think there'll be anything in the body – anything to prove that he didn't commit suicide? Any other sort of drug?'

'The post-mortem is tomorrow morning. We'll know then. But I doubt it. Perry wouldn't have made that blunder.'

'You'll want me at the inquest?'

'Certainly not. But you can go and have a look at the post-mortem if you like. It'll suit your ghoulish instincts.' There was an irritable edge to his voice.

'Take it easy,' said Casson. Strutt shrugged and came back to his desk.

'All right. All right. But this sort of murder boils me up. I don't mind the chap who loses his temper and takes an axe to his old woman. That's human folly. I abominate these cold, skilful jobs. Bah!'

'Why don't you want me at the inquest?'

'Perry may be there. I don't want him to see you. He mustn't know you are mixed up in this.'

'Surely he won't dare attend?'

'He may. He'll want to know what the verdict is, how the body was found, and all that sort of thing. Besides, there's no danger in it. If he's spotted, he has the perfect story. He knew Macfarlane. He was with him that night. He wouldn't be stupid enough to deny it. If he were questioned, he would probably even put the final stitch in his alibi by saying that Macfarlane threatened to commit suicide and he tried to argue him out of it. He'll reckon he's dead safe.'

'Suppose the Coroner returns a verdict of murder?'

'He won't. He'll just find the cause of death. It'll be an open verdict. There'll be no evidence of fingerprints. And I've fixed the char – what's her name – Queenleigh to say that it was she who found the stiff.' He chuckled without humour. 'I told her it was marked in the web of destiny or some such rot, and she gave me another long lecture on the Stars and agreed to do it. So that'll leave you out.'

'What part are you planning for me?' Casson asked gently. Strutt squinted at him.

'You are the only person who is near to Perry.'

'I'm not that intimate . . .'

'You'll do. Somehow you've got to get him. You've got to keep up this game of living in Bickersteth Street and drinking beer with the little swine.'

'Yes,' said Casson thoughtfully. 'I will indeed. It will be a pleasure to see him hanged.'

'You may not catch him,' Strutt said as if he were talking to a precocious child. 'I rather doubt it. But you're all we've got and we've got to use you.'

'Thank you,' Casson replied. 'You are so courteous.'

Strutt grinned.

'Set a madman to catch a madman,' he remarked.

Casson gazed out of the window at the soft, lovely evening sky while Strutt fiddled with a pencil.

'What about the girl?' Casson asked.

'I've told you. She doesn't know, or she won't talk.'

'I mean, is she safe? Won't Perry turn on her next? After all, he won't know how much young Macfarlane had told her.'

'She's as safe as a house. It's obvious that Perry killed the boy for one of two reasons: either Macfarlane wanted to quit and get married and have done with crime; or else he wanted to tell his girl friend. Perry couldn't afford either, because either way the girl would get to know, and he couldn't trust her not to talk. So he tried to argue Macfarlane out of it and then, when the boy proved obstinate, he croaked him. But he was pretty certain that the girl knew nothing when Macfarlane was killed because the argument between Perry and Macfarlane was still going on. We know that from the chap who followed them on the night Mac was killed. Therefore Mac had not yet split to his girl. She's all right.'

'Umm.'

'You're not convinced?'

'No. There's something missing somewhere.'

'There is,' Strutt replied briskly. 'A conviction for murder. That's all.'

Casson rose to go. As he did so he pulled a long envelope out of his inside pocket.

'Here's my statement,' he said. 'I'll sign it now and you can witness it.'

'Good. Sign away, my boy.' Strutt was becoming genial, and with a flutter of excitement Casson recognized the sign. When Strutt was genial on a job he was at his most dangerous.

'One more thing,' said the fat policeman as Casson was walking to the door. 'You might like to try your charms on young Miss Shaw. If she thinks you're the film-star type she might cry on your shoulder. Though I don't give a damn how much she cries so long as she talks.' He sighed. 'I'm afraid I'm not the right shape. She took one look at me and shut up like a clam.'

'You dazzled her,' Casson remarked and shut the door.

But Casson waited till the day of the inquest to make his visit to Jean Shaw. He reckoned that she would have taken the day off from work to attend the Coroner's Court and would be sitting alone at home that afternoon, miserably idle, beginning to realize in its fullness what had happened to her life.

He took the Rolls out to Putney, driving slowly and lazily through the hot sunshine which scorched the soft tar on the roads and glittered off the pavements. Disraeli Road was deserted, decently somnolent, its tall, detached houses made to lose some of their normal Victorian pomposity and to look almost raffish in the overburdening gaiety of light.

A tall, heavy-boned woman of about fifty opened the door to him. Her mouth was unemotional and determined. She wore a plait round her head and only a plain, thick gold wedding ring on her left hand.

'Miss Shaw is indisposed,' she replied to Casson's question. There was a Scots inflexion in her voice. 'I am afraid she will be receiving no visitors.'

'It is a police matter,' he said. She hesitated.

'Very well. Come in. You had better see her in the parlour.'

The parlour was too clean to be comfortable. Its ordered spickness forbade sitting down. There was a grand piano with a shawl over it and there were water-colour paintings of the Western Isles. He lit a cigarette and sighed.

Jean Shaw was quite attractive but not pretty. She had steady, grey eyes and fine, brown hair. Her complexion was good and she used little make-up. He would not have picked her out in a crowd. Her voice, when she spoke, was modulated also by the same Scots intonation, but in her it was more pronounced than in the coarser voice of the woman who had answered the door.

She sat down on the edge of the sofa, her hands in her lap, looking at him.

'I am sorry, but I have told you everything I can,' she said.

'So the police thought.'

'You are not a policeman?' She stood up. Casson shook his head. Her right hand was plucking at the button on her black suit.

'You are a journalist?'

He smiled.

'Please sit down, Miss Shaw,' he said. 'I am not a journalist. Nor am I a policeman. But I am working with the police on this case of Jim Macfarlane.'

'Case?'

'Yes, Miss Shaw. Do you believe that Jim committed suicide?'

'It was not in his nature. I'm sure Jim would never . . .' She turned away from him.

'Exactly,' he continued. 'I do not believe it either. I believe that Jim Macfarlane was murdered.'

She turned back to him, staring.

'Murdered?'

'Yes.'

'But – but why? No one would have wanted to – to kill Jim. He never harmed anybody. He couldn't.'

Casson looked round for an ashtray. He wanted to catch her off guard. She rose and fetched a small china plate from the mantelpiece.

'I shall have to wash this after you,' she observed with a faint smile. 'Mrs Ogilvy never has them used.'

As she was bending down to give him the ashtray, Casson said:

'Jim was murdered because he knew a criminal.'

She straightened up and stared at him. The words seemed at first to have no meaning for her.

'A criminal? Jim? Oh no. It couldn't have been.'

'What couldn't have been?'

'Jim knowing someone like that. He just wouldn't.' She sat

E   129

down again on the edge of the sofa, and looked fixedly at her feet.

'What had Jim done?' she asked.

'Nothing,' he lied.

'Then why – I don't understand. . . .'

He broke in on her.

'We want to catch the man who murdered him, Miss Shaw. We think you can help. I want you to tell me everything that happened between you and Jim during the last fortnight of his life. Will you? Please?'

'I have already told the police everything I know,' she said, without looking up.

'Somewhere,' he persisted, 'there may be a tiny clue – something he said or did which you wouldn't think important, something which we can fit into the picture of his murder.'

'No,' she said stubbornly. 'I am afraid not. And I do not believe that he was murdered.'

He tried again.

'Miss Shaw, a man has been killed. Unless we find the murderer, another man may die. If that happened, the responsibility for the second death might be yours as well as ours. We have got to find the killer.'

Her face was pale but composed.

'How do I know who you are?' she asked.

He smiled.

'You don't. You're a sensible girl to ask. I have no warrant card, but if you telephone the police officer who saw you he will tell you that he knows me. You remember his name?'

'Superintendent Strutt.'

'In the telephone book you will find the number of the West End Central Police Station. Ring it and ask for Strutt. Ask him if he knows Casson Duker and if he is satisfied that I should be here.'

The steady gaze continued to look at him. Then it faltered and fell away before his.

'I cannot believe Jim was murdered,' she insisted. 'It's too senseless.'

'He was,' replied Casson. 'Will you tell me everything?'

She hesitated.

'Jim and I quarrelled before – before he died.'

'People in love often quarrel,' he said gently. Her voice was shaking when she answered him.

'We had been quarrelling for – oh, it seemed ages. It was a nightmare. There was nothing I could do to stop it. He went on and on, and I couldn't say I was sorry because I wasn't.'

'What was the quarrel about?' His pulses were hammering.

She looked straight at him and said defiantly:

'Jim said I was a wanton.'

There was a pause.

'What?' Casson said.

She did not reply.

'God Almighty,' he said. 'It's wicked.'

'Thank you for disbelieving it,' she replied. 'Jim wouldn't. He accused me of – of going with other men. I thought he was joking. Then I got angry and refused to see him. He only said that proved I was guilty. It was terrible. I thought he was over-working and tried to get him to see a doctor. He said that was a ruse to get away from me. Then he got pompous about – about being chaste and lectured me; and dear Jim could be a wee bit pompous sometimes.' She smiled sadly.

'It's monstrous,' Casson breathed. The girl seemed almost calm, sure of herself, as reserved as ever. But he could sense the pressure of pain which she was holding down inside her and he wished that she would cry.

'Did he give you any reason for his accusations?' Casson asked, leaning forward.

'He said that I had been to the pictures with another man. He told me the day and the time. He was quite right. I went with Mrs Ogilvy's nephew. He travels in clocks and he used to know my family in Scotland. That's why I live here. I've been out several times with him. He's a nice, quiet man. When I told Jim that, he laughed. He just laughed.'

'But did Jim see you at the pictures?'

'No. A friend of his saw us. Or so Jim said. I'm sure Jim wouldn't have spied on me.'

'Who was the friend?' Casson leaned further forward. He knew the friend's name but he wanted to hear her say it.

'I don't know. He wouldn't tell me. He said the friend regretted ever mentioning that he had seen me.'

Casson imagined Perry looking as if he regretted it even while he spun his net of lies. His mouth was dry with anger.

'But nothing else?' Casson urged. 'Nothing that Jim mentioned as unusual? No upset that he'd had – apart from all this nonsense?'

She thought for a time. Then she smiled again her sad, swiftly vanishing smile.

'It's cruel, really, now I come to think of it,' she said. 'Jim was jealous of me. But before that he had told me a story of a friend of his in the City being jealous – or rather being upset about women. And Jim said then how silly men could be.'

'Did he tell you any more?'

'He said he had been having lunch with this man in the City – it was a friend he quite often had lunch with, I believe – and he told him that he had seen him some days before with a lady. Jim had been coming back from his morning coffee and his friend was outside the bank with a lady who was a customer at the bank and Jim pulled his leg about rich lady customers lending him money. But his friend went as white as a sheet' – vividly Casson recollected Strutt's description from the police report of Perry and Macfarlane together in their City snack-bar and all too clearly he understood what had happened – 'and told him to mind his own business and not to be a Nosey Parker. Jim was quite hurt about it at the time but then he saw how silly it all was.'

'Do you remember when you went to the pictures with Mrs Ogilvy's nephew?'

'I've been quite often.'

'But the last time?'

She frowned.

'It was the night before Jim and I had our row – when he accused me. No. It was two nights before.'

'Perry was lucky,' said Casson grimly. 'He caught you the first time he tried. Did Jim tell you the name of his friend in the City?'

'No.'

'Did he ever mention the name of Perry? John Henry Perry? Of Hammersmith?'

132

'No.'

'Perry was the friend.'

'You know him?'

'Yes. Perry is a blackmailer. And now I know exactly what happened. Perry used your Jim to give him information from the Bank. Jim did not know that Perry was a criminal. All he knew was that Perry was an old member of the bank's staff. He saw no harm in gossiping to him. The rich lady customer was one of Perry's victims. I could tell you her name but I won't. Perry thought that Jim might spoil his game if he told other people in the bank whom he had seen Perry with and if they got to hear ultimately that she had been blackmailed.

'He followed you until you went out with another man. That's his technique. He was lucky. He only had to follow you once. Do you remember being followed?'

She shook her head.

'I wouldn't even think about it. Why should I?'

'Perry told Jim that you were unfaithful. He worked him up to the state where Jim tormented himself with your supposed wantonness, into a state in which one might presume him to have committed suicide. Perry even got him to go to a doctor and get a sleeping draught. That draught put Jim to sleep while Perry turned on the gas. Perry murdered Jim.'

She was looking at him, deeply troubled.

'I can't believe it.'

'I'm sure of it. Everything fits. I know it is true. To begin with we thought Jim was his accomplice ...'

She flushed.

'You couldn't think that.'

Casson shrugged.

'People do queer things,' he remarked. 'Even criminals sometimes look honest.'

'You are sure it – it happened like that?'

'Quite sure. I am sorry but I am quite sure.'

'Then you will arrest him?'

Casson stood up.

'Miss Shaw,' he said gravely, 'we have no evidence on which to arrest him.'

133

Her face was set.

'He died distrusting me,' she whispered.

'He did. He died thinking that you were a wanton.'

She looked up at him.

'But you *will* arrest him?'

'In time.'

He stood up to go.

'I must ask you not to repeat this, Miss Shaw,' he said. 'It is very important that the murderer thinks he is safe.'

'I am not likely to want to tell anybody,' she replied and for the first time he heard desolation in her voice. Then she said in a whisper, not looking at him:

'And you know he was so kind. He wouldn't hurt anyone – except me, and that was by mistake. He once found a kitten in that bombed bit by St Paul's and took it home and was terribly upset for a time when it grew up and went away. And he didn't really like cats at all.'

'Thank you, Miss Shaw,' said Casson softly, and left her.

He closed the door behind him and waited, holding his breath to hear whether she would fling herself on the sofa and weep. He prayed that she would lose her self-control and give way and thus obtain a temporary peace. All he heard was a soft thumping as she patted the cushions back into shape.

He drove to Savile Row at a dangerous speed. He ran up the stairs to Strutt's office and flung open the door. Strutt was sitting in his shirt-sleeves, reading a long type-written report. He looked up with a frown as Casson came in and slammed the door.

'So ruddy what?' he began.

'We're wrong,' said Casson. 'Macfarlane was innocent. To his last moment he didn't know that Perry was a crook. Perry bitched up his engagement and then killed him just in case – just in case he suspected. Just in case! We're so wrong that you ought to be fired and I ought to be shot. And if Perry burns in Hell for eternity I shall laugh.'

'Sit down,' said Strutt.

Casson told him the story. When he had finished the two men looked at each other. Slowly Strutt let out his breath.

'All right,' he said. 'All right. All right. I'll get him. By God, I will. I'll have him followed every hour of the day and night, and somehow we'll get him the . . .'

'Yes,' Casson interrupted. 'That will help.'

Strutt leered at him.

'Help? It won't ruddy help if he doesn't do anything. I want a hanging verdict, not a study of social conditions in Hammersmith.'

'It will help me,' Casson observed.

'I don't want to help you,' Strutt bawled. 'Blast you, what do you think this is – the Salvation Army?'

Strutt's expression changed when he heard the tone of voice in which Casson said:

'I am going to frighten Perry into hanging himself.'

Chapter Twelve

JOHN PERRY leant on the rail of Chiswick Mall and watched a river-steamer sliding downstream towards Putney. With contempt he looked at the anonymous black figures of the people who packed the decks. Sizzling fools, he thought, as the sunlight glared on the water and intensified the sound of music from the boat.

Sweaty fools, he thought; making inane conversation under an awning and all smelling! He had always loathed them, their loud voices and tennis clubs and school ties and dirty stories. They were always busy, always talking, always making the same silly jokes.

And, for all their loud talk, not one of them had killed a man. But he had. He, John Perry, had deliberately and carefully and successfully killed his man. He had put a world between himself and those noisy middle-class louts, a world of daring and unique accomplishment.

It was true that some of them had killed Germans and Japs in the last war; but that was not heroic. They had killed under orders. They had killed because it was cowardly not to kill, killed because they were frightened. As he had always said, they were cowards at heart. Only he had dared to face the heaviest penalty that the State could devise. And he had dared it in order to guard his own private and personal ambitions. That was courage for you, real heroic courage, the sort that would have been appreciated by the Romans. That was the height, to kill for what you believed to be beautiful.

The loud-voiced oafs in the public-house would say that murder was a bad thing: which only showed that they could not think straight. What, after all, was the difference between Englishmen killing Germans in order to safeguard England and he, John Perry, killing Macfarlane in order to safeguard his own liberty? To the logical thinker there was no difference. And I am logical, said John Perry to himself. I have killed logically and I have got away with it. It's easy if you think it out.

136

And what a success it had been. It was only a pity that he could not boast about it in some select circle of men who would recognize their own difference from the common mob in the streets, and who would not be shocked by any peculiar means which their friends took to preserve their own happiness. In such a circle they could freely discuss murder; discuss it without any of the fal-lals of thought which confused the middle classes. They would begin, perhaps, by discussing even perversions, or intoxicating experiments with drugs: anything in fact that could lead them to the fine states of mind which were the only purpose in life. And he could tell them that he had achieved that end many months ago with his private collection and his quiet dedication to a life lived alone among his self-satisfactions. Just as quietly would he announce that he had killed to preserve his independence: and round that select circle would run a ripple of involuntary and well-bred admiration.

Perry shifted his position, taking the weight off the left foot with its painful blister. The river was now bare and whitely empty and he gazed at it vacantly, playing with the pleasurable anticipation of what he would buy next. Two hundred and fifty pounds he had got from that silly General's wife. A hundred and fifty of that would go towards his living expenses for the next six months, until after Christmas, by which time he would be ready for another *coup*. That left one hundred for something of marble or wood or, this time perhaps, of ormulu. It would be nice to have a clock – Louis XV or XVI period – to put on the mantelpiece between the George II candlesticks. For a hundred pounds you could probably get quite a good one. If not he would have to dip into his reserves. He knew little about clocks, and wondered if a hundred pounds would be enough.

His mind picked up the memory of that morning when he had gone into Oxford from Abingdon, where he was holidaying, and had wandered round the Ashmolean Museum, intent on the Roman statues. He had gone on upstairs to see if there were any more of the splendid sarcophagi, but he had forgotten the search in his excitement at seeing a case full of old watches. Dozens of them hung there, all stopped, as if time was of no importance to them – or to him either – and as if, together, they had escaped the dull, daily round into a timeless universe of jewellery and enamel and figured silver.

His stomach rumbled and, automatically, he reached for his watch. Time for dinner. Ten minutes after midday. He stood up and stretched his shoulders. He felt rather good. Perhaps he would celebrate and open a tin of his favourite soft roes; and have them on toast. Not on fried bread – that would be too rich.

He moved away from the hot rail on which he had been leaning. Then he jerked, as though hit by an electric current, and turned back quickly towards the river. His stomach felt icy cold and unpleasantly queasy. A uniformed policeman had turned the corner of the road behind him and was patrolling slowly up the Mall.

Perry tried to control himself. It must have been the suddenness of it, he thought. It was ridiculous to be so upset at the sight of an ordinary, cloddish policeman. He, Perry, was a cut above such fears. His killing had been perfect and he had nothing to fear. He must get used to controlling himself.

He stayed in the sunlight for five minutes, then turned away sedately home. He did not feel the same enthusiasm for soft roes, and contented himself with bread and cheese, cocoa, and some pickles. While he ate he drew comfort from the meditations of Marcus Aurelius.

On the other side of Bickersteth Street, Casson was sitting in his bedroom, watching Perry's house. The camera and tripod had gone. It was now a matter of human calculations, his mind against another man's, a gamble on psychological prediction. He was still unsure of the strength of Perry's mind and the tensility of his self-control. How long would the game go on?

'They never last out,' Strutt had said the day before.

'Not even if he thinks he has committed a foolproof murder?' Casson had countered.

'Never. They haven't got the stamina.'

'They can't bear the load of guilt?'

Strutt had snorted.

'Guilt! Murderers don't have a sense of guilt. What the hell do you think they are – devout Methodists?'

'Then you think that their memory isn't sufficiently strong?'

'Whatever that may mean.'

'I mean, that they can't be sure that they haven't committed some mistake. They can't remember any mistakes, but they fear their memory has let them down. They're afraid they may have mucked it, in some way they can't remember. So they work their memory to shreds trying to remember and reassure themselves? And the more they try the less use it is because the memory gets blurred. So they end up in a state of jitters?'

'More or less. Only the intelligent ones. The other ones are apes. They're either so stupid they know they'll never be caught or they're so stupid that they know they will.'

'But this one is different?'

Strutt expressed his view of Perry in two scornful obscenities.

'It's all arranged, then,' Casson had said. 'You leave the little man alone until I see how his mind is working. I'll play him along as a friend and gauge the texture of his fear. Then your boys'll start. Then we'll build the fear up. All right?'

'All right. But don't be too long with your high-flown psychological researches. I want to hang the runt, not read his autobiography.'

They had taken a police car and gone down to the Chiswick Police Station. Strutt had introduced Casson to the Superintendent, the C.I.D. Inspector, and his two plain-clothes Sergeants. After the plan of action had been discussed two young uniformed constables had been brought in. They had been briefed and only waited for the word to go.

Casson moved restlessly in his chair and once again picked up a worn newspaper cutting. For the fourth time he read through the report on the inquest. 'Broken Romance', it was headed and her name was mentioned. Miss Jean Shaw of Putney gave evidence that she and her fiancé had frequently quarrelled. He was of a jealous disposition, she had admitted. The Coroner had thanked her for her evidence and had found the bare fact of death: '. . . asphyxia from coal-gas poisoning.' That was all.

Miss Jean Shaw of Putney. She disliked him, that Casson knew. And women who disliked him also fascinated him. Nevertheless this article was a bit much. It was piling unpleasantness on suffering.

But Strutt had been adamant. He had insisted on getting a report in to the papers.

'It'll save her from Perry,' Strutt had said. 'After that evidence she'll be as safe as a Chubb lock. There'll be no need for him to go after her. And what's more, he'll know he's safe himself and that his murder is assumed to be suicide. So he'll be cock-a-hoop, and the jolt will be twice as bitter when he finds he isn't so safe as he ruddy well thought.'

'But if he comes to the inquest he'll hear it all there,' Casson had objected. 'You don't have to splash it all over the papers.'

'He may not come. And I want to be sure he knows. I want to be doubly sure of everything until he swings.'

'Think of the girl. The poor kid's in Purgatory as it is.'

'You think of her. I haven't the time. I'm thinking of Perry, and I'm going to get him if it breaks me. As it probably will unless you do your stuff.'

Casson dropped the cutting and kicked it under the table. She was a nice girl, was Miss Shaw, and there was a lot of warmth in her if you could only bring it out. She'd make a wonderful wife – if you wanted a wife.

At that moment Perry came out of his house, locked the door, and strolled up the street. Casson followed. It was a dull walk. Perry strolled up to King Street, turned left and then left again. He went slowly down to Chiswick Mall and leant on the rail. For about twenty minutes he seemed to be watching the boats on the river. Then, at tea-time, he returned home.

Casson was only intrigued because it seemed out of Perry's routine. He never went for a stroll; or, at least, he never had done so before. Did it mean that he was restless? Could it mean that he was too worried to stay in his house, and had to damp down his thoughts by walking?

But in the Shepley Arms that evening he was the same as usual, clean, prim, and reserved. Casson, as a matter of course, took his pint over and joined Perry in his corner. They chatted in a desultory way, and Casson was interested to note that Perry accepted a sherry after his beer, and did not look at his watch to see whether it were time for him to go home.

Perry sipped his sherry, put the tall glass down carefully, wiped his mouth, and said:

'Do you know anything about clocks?'

'Not much,' Casson replied. 'I had a friend who was a bit of an enthusiast. Why?'

'I thought of purchasing one – an old one, of course.'

'To add to your charming collection?'

'Yes. My mantelpiece needs something to fill it.'

Casson sighed with envy.

'You are a lucky fellow,' he observed. 'I'd give a good deal to have a collection like that. So would a lot of my friends. It must have cost a mint of money to build up?'

Perry took another sip of his sherry.

'I bought judiciously,' he replied. 'I have some private means, you see.' The hell you have, thought Casson. Loot from Lockyer, loot from Mrs Gordonstoun. 'I proposed to go up to the West End of London tomorrow and look around for a clock,' Perry continued. 'Would you care to accompany me?'

Casson paused. He must not be too accommodating. Then he replied casually:

'I've got to finish an article tomorrow. But the next day's free for me. I think it would be rather amusing.'

'I could make that convenient,' said Perry. He fell silent, gazing across the room. Abruptly he finished his sherry, got up and left. Casson nodded good night.

Perry never moved the next day. Only the net curtains flapping in the fitful breeze showed that there was someone in 51 Bickersteth Street to air the house. The windows were shut at five o'clock in the evening, and that was that. Casson kept away from the Shepley Arms.

Their joint outing to the West End was a macabre one. While they walked up and down the streets of Mayfair – Bury Street, Duke Street, Albemarle, and Dover Street – looking into shop windows in the plate glass of which Casson could see the reflection of Perry's covetous eyes, he felt that he was alien to the people who walked the same pavements. He imagined they knew that he was looking at clocks in the company of a murderer, but they held their peace and glanced slyly at him as they passed by. They knew, but they were saying nothing. They were waiting for the news to be announced in the evening papers. They were waiting for Perry to be arrested by a solid, blue policeman. Then the news would be printed and safe. Until then, their eyes slipped over the two men and moved quickly on.

Casson laughed at the folly of his thoughts, laughed out loud.

'What's up?' Perry asked, turning back from the shop window into which he was gazing.

Casson gestured.

'You see all these people. How little they know of each other. One might be a millionaire and another a criminal. That man with the pince-nez might be going bankrupt this evening or deceiving his wife this afternoon, and that woman over there in the brown hat might be a baby-farmer. You just don't know what the next person is like. They might as well be alone in separate universes.'

Perry glanced at him.

'Yes,' he said.

They walked again, up the Burlington Arcade. Casson was in torment lest Perry insisted on going into a shop in which he, Casson, was a well-known customer. But Perry was cautious. He scrutinized the clocks and looked at their tags. Twice he went in by himself to ask the price.

'They're expensive,' he commented as he emerged from the second shop. 'I shall wait until I see what there is in the sales.'

Casson was anxious not to lose this opportunity of being with Perry for a whole day.

'There's another shop in Knightsbridge,' he suggested. 'Very well known. They've got some wonderful stuff there. Let's stroll along and see.'

'Very good. But I'd like to go down to Charles II Street again. One there really took my fancy.'

For a long time Perry looked at the clock, then he shook his head and turned away.

'Not exactly what I want,' he said. The two men walked through St James's Square into St James's Street, and Perry turned up the street towards Piccadilly.

'What about strolling through the Park by the Palace?' Casson suggested desperately.

'I'd like to walk up St James's Street, if you don't mind,' Perry replied.

The journey was a nightmare to Casson. At any moment he might meet a friend coming out of one of the Clubs, and the chance mention of his real name would finish him with Perry. His spirits lightened as they passed Boodles' and crossed Jermyn Street, but fell again when Perry insisted on standing in front of White's and gazing up at its windows. Casson hoped fervently that Roddy Lape would not be standing behind that tall ground-floor window with his usual double brandy in his hand: and, if he were, that he would not wave to him.

'Very nice,' said Perry, still gazing at the splendid façade. 'I suppose all the persons in there are very rich? Do you have to have a lot of money to join?'

'Not exactly,' said Casson.

'I should like to belong to such a place,' said Perry boldly. Casson was so startled that he could not reply. He could just imagine Perry in, for example, Cane's, moving like a prim and voracious lamprey between the pillars and the pictures. And supposing he were asked by Perry to put him up for membership! The impossible humour of it struck him so forcibly that he felt for a moment contented.

As they walked on, his mind became occupied with this new aspect of Perry. He had never suspected that the little man's ambitions were social as well as acquisitive. To blackmail, and in the end to kill, for snobbery was a repulsive comment on the human mind. To do those things for silver candlesticks, he could comprehend. But to kill for a handshake was ludicrous, ten-dimensional, a music-hall joke.

He shivered in the sunlight that was flooding into Piccadilly between the Ritz and the Berkeley. When you were faced by the abyss over which the human mind hung poised, then you got vertigo. You got the height sickness that urged you to throw yourself over and end the intolerable strain of clinging to your balance. And you got nausea, too, when you saw the things which moved with rustling, unclean wings in the jagged depths.

Casson broke the thread of his thoughts and bought all the afternoon papers. As he glanced through them he saw that his luck held. The *Standard* carried a story of the arrest of a safe-breaking gang. He held the paper out to Perry and indicated the headline.

'You see,' he said. 'They always get caught. I never understand why criminals do it. They always make some mistake.'

Perry read the article, standing stiffly in the middle of the pavement while the trees of the Green Park rustled over his head. He handed the paper back to Casson and they moved on again.

'You only read about the ones who get caught,' he remarked. 'I expect there are some who get away with it, the clever ones.'

'Never,' Casson replied emphatically. 'They're stupid, the whole lot of them. If they weren't stupid, they would add up the odds against their being successful, and they would go into business instead. But they always think they are cleverer than the rest, and they never are.'

'There must be exceptions?'

'No. I'll tell you why. They lose control.'

'Do they?'

'They lose control while they are doing their crime. That is to say, they lose clarity of thought. They make a slip. They forget about it. And the police get them. You know?'

Perry stopped and stared at Casson.

'Eh?'

Casson stopped too.

'What do you mean?'

Perry went on:

'I don't know anything about it,' he said. 'Crime doesn't interest me.'

Here we are, thought Casson, both spinning our fishing-nets of lies round each other, one to save his life and the other to take it. And Perry must have had something to drink with Macfarlane on the night when he killed him. He couldn't have been sure of his clarity during the murder.

They walked in silence. Casson pointed out the colour of Apsley House, comparing it to Montacute and Stanway, but Perry did not reply. He seemed absorbed in his thoughts. When they got to Knightsbridge he stopped suddenly, said he had done enough for the day, mumbled good-bye, and disappeared down the steps of the Underground.

Humming a tune, Casson watched him go. Perry had shown that his self-control was not perfect. He had allowed himself to get rattled, to be knocked off balance. If those few moments of uncertainty festered, if he were forced by fear to ransack his memory again and again to make sure that he had not slipped up, then the sweetness of Macfarlane's murder would become a repeated sourness in his mouth. Thinking of Greenhaugh, Jean Shaw, and Macfarlane, Casson had no pity on him.

He went into a call-box and telephoned Strutt.

'I've got him quaking,' Casson said when the Superintendent came on the phone. 'You can try the Dramatic Society.'

'Good boy,' Strutt answered. 'I'll tell them to turn the heat on tonight.'

'Too early,' Casson objected. 'Let him simmer down and regain confidence. Give him twenty-four hours. He'll be feeling better tomorrow. When he's got a bit of balance back we can undo it again, and that should rock him a bit more.'

'All right. Tomorrow. Good work.'

'So long.'

'I say . . .'

'Yes?'

'Is that little swine really sweating?' Strutt sounded hopeful.

'Not yet. Not enough.'

'Pity. I'd enjoy my supper more if I thought he was having a horrid time. Good-bye.'

Casson dozed the next morning and afternoon and sat by the open window waiting for the long summer day to end. The sunset was interminably violet. Blatantly it lingered. But at last darkness seeped along the street and, from two Squares away, the church clock struck eleven. He sat on until the next single half-hour stroke chimed. Then he let himself out of the house, crossed Bickersteth Street, and stationed himself on the other side, a few paces up the intersection round the corner from No. 51.

He did not need to stand there long. At ten to twelve precisely he heard the regular, metronomic tread of a policeman, approaching at standard pace. The footsteps stopped. There was a sharp, repeated cough. Casson moved forward and peered round the corner.

Under the lamplight was the blue uniform. An innocent, rather pink, face was fixedly regarding the roof of Perry's house. Casson chuckled. It was the younger of the two uniformed constables whom he had met at the Chiswick Station – Police Constable Bentley, 'F' Division's crack quarter-miler.

The constable appeared to make up his mind. He moved ponderously up the garden path to the door of No. 51. After the heavy rat-tat on the knocker, silence fell again, broken only by P.C. Bentley's breathing and then yet another echoing rat-tat. Casson heard the scrape of a withdrawn bolt.

'Very sorry, sir,' said Constable Bentley. 'Thought I saw a man on your roof. Thought it might be a burglar. Have you heard anything, sir?'

'No,' said Perry. 'Nothing at all.'

'Think I'd better just have a dekko, sir. Otherwise there might be a nasty accident, you know. You don't mind if I come in, sir?'

'I assure you, Officer, that I have heard nothing,' objected Perry. 'I am certain that everything is quite safe.'

'Better make sure, sir. That's the motto of the police, sir. Always make sure.' Casson hugged himself with delight. Constable Bentley was an excellent actor. 'Now if you'd be good enough to let me, sir, I'll just have a quick look round.'

'I assure you, Officer, that I'm perfectly safe,' Perry insisted.

'No one is ever perfectly safe,' Bentley replied heartily. 'Besides, sir, if there were a burglar, which I think there is, you wouldn't want to keep me out of your house, would you? You'd be compounding a felony.'

The door squeaked slightly as it opened, then slammed shut. The street returned to silence. Casson had moved out from his sheltering wall to watch the flashing of lights in room after room of Perry's private museum. The front door squeaked again.

'Much obliged to you, sir,' said Constable Bentley. 'Glad there was nothing. You've got some classy stuff there, sir, if I may say so. You want to take care of that. Must be worth a lot, I dare say. Tell you what, Mr Perry, I'll tell the lads, and they'll keep an eye on the house to see you don't get anyone pinching anything. . . .'

'That's quite all right, Officer,' Perry broke in. 'Please don't trouble to keep an eye on the house.'

'Better be certain, sir,' Bentley replied with apparent goodwill.

'I assure you . . .' Perry began.

'Good night, sir,' Bentley interrupted. The heavy boots moved off, the weight of their tread a trifle exaggerated. Without doubt Bentley's success had gone to his head and he was beginning to ham the part.

The boots stopped. Casson, from an angle, safe in the darkness, looked down Bickersteth Street. Bentley stood on the far side of the street, watching Perry's house. There was a faint noise of a curtain being pulled back in one of the windows of No. 51. Perry must have seen Bentley, for it was swiftly drawn again.

On the day after, Perry turned up in the Shepley Arms as usual, but, for the first time since Casson had known him, he looked tired. His eyes were puffy and the whites in the inner corner of his eyes were bloodshot.

He bought his pint and came over to sit by Casson. For a time he said nothing. Then casually he asked:

'Did you hear a row last night?'

'Row? No. Why?'

'A policeman knocked me up about midnight and said he'd seen a burglar on my roof. He insisted on going into every room to see that everything was all right. I was most annoyed. He was a very inquisitive man.'

'They're curious by nature,' said Casson reassuringly. 'They'll sniff anything to see whether it smells.' His reply did not seem particularly welcome.

'Don't you think its unpardonable?' Perry insisted. 'They can't just come into your house like that.'

'You know how it is. The poor fellows have got to stop crime somehow. And, by and large, they're pretty efficient, so far as one can gather.'

Perry lapsed into a sombre silence. He finished his beer before his usual forty minutes were up, refused another, and got up to leave.

'If you're not busy tomorrow,' said Casson, 'it might interest you to come along with me. I'm going to Chiswick House to look at the stuff they've got there. I believe there are some outstanding William and Mary chairs.'

'I don't think I will,' Perry replied, rather ungraciously. 'I don't really feel like it.'

'I wish you would. I'd like your advice. I may want to use some of their stuff for my book.'

Perry hesitated.

'Very well,' he said. 'Eleven tomorrow morning.'

Casson went to Cane's for dinner and rang Strutt from the Club.

'Hullo, hullo,' said Strutt. 'Have you broken him?'

'Not yet. But the Dramatic Society was superb. My congratulations to Constable Bentley.'

Strutt growled.

'I'll see he has a good kick up the rump, in case he gets a swollen head. Is Perry shaken?'

'He's going.'

'Going. You mean he's skipped? Curse you.'

'Relax,' said Casson. 'Of course he hasn't skipped. And he won't skip.'

'I wish I was as cocky about it as you are.'

'You sound like a man with a hangover. What's up?'

'I am, blast you. I've been up all last night and I'm still up. And if you don't get Perry soon I'll be up a ruddy gum tree. Every time I think of that little crawler it makes my guts turn over.'

'They won't turn for long. He and I are going to Chiswick House tomorrow morning. At eleven. That's the time for the next set of fireworks. The boys can pick us up in Burlington Lane or Chiswick Lane. Can you fix it?'

'Of course I can fix it. Do you think I'm a paralysed choirboy?'

'And lay on the show for just after twelve. We don't want to be kept waiting or he may bolt.'

Strutt chuckled.

'I'll get them to pull in every pimp in Chiswick. You wait till you get there!'

Chapter Thirteen

CASSON finished his lamb chops and sat on for a long time in the dining-room of Cane's, nursing between his hands his second glass of Gevrey Chambertin. He was brooding over the few moves still left in the game. He was convinced that he and Strutt could drive Perry into a state of desperation. But would that be far enough? Would it be sufficient to disintegrate the cold little man's sense of self-preservation? He did not know. All he knew from his experiences in the Airborne Division was that one could not predict the behaviour of the human being *in extremis*.

He ordered a glass of brandy and took it into the deserted smoking-room. Lying back in the huge leather armchair, his mind reflected every separate aspect of the problem until he realized that he had overlooked the essential point. He could soften Perry by fear. But the way to hang him was by conceit. In the end it must be the strength of distortion in Perry's character that would convict him; and Casson was now convinced that the strongest distortion in him was snobbery. If that ambition could be inflated it would burst him.

Casson finished his brandy and returned to Bickersteth Street. It was deserted, the windows of its houses still lidless and diseased with moonlight. He went straight to bed and to sleep.

For the second night running Perry lay awake. He lay rigidly on his back, as he was used to doing. His eyes were tightly closed, but, behind them, his mind was whirling in a fixed circle.

That Police Officer could only have wanted to see if there had really been a burglar. He looked too young and too innocent to conceal any other purpose. But why had he insisted in going all over the house? Was he just blunderingly curious like the young are: like Macfarlane was? He had the same type of face, too: pink and white and innocent.

Perry switched on the light. He tipped two aspirins into his hand, hesitated, and let them slip back into the bottle. He hated drugs. He had never taken them, and he would not admit the need to take them now. If you took a drug it meant that you were getting out of control: and that he could not, dare not, allow. He had chosen his way and he would go through with it, carefully, deliberately, logically. So long as he stuck to the first principles of safety he was unbeatable.

He turned over on to his side, trying to find sleep. But all his life he had only slept on his back, and the change of position made him even more awake. For a fleeting moment he wished that he had a sleeping draught like Macfarlane's. Knocked you out quick, he had been told.

He couldn't have forgotten anything in that flat? He had checked that there was no string left in the mat where he had pulled it up against the door. Had one of the two pieces fallen out of his pocket? He remembered counting them when he got home. They were safe. He had checked on the handkerchief also. What else could there have been?

He switched on the light and took two aspirins. At all costs he must sleep. It was just a temporary fit of nerves. His stomach was upset. He would feel better tomorrow. Besides, there was nothing else he could have left behind in the flat. And even if there had been fingerprints, they wouldn't matter. He would frankly admit to having been a friend of Macfarlane's. They couldn't upset the story of a clever man who kept his head.

If he were questioned he could tell the truth with a clear conscience. Except, of course, for turning on the gas-tap and pulling the mat against the bedroom door and forcing the tipsy young man to take his sleeping draught. Thank goodness Macfarlane hadn't been sick and vomited it up. That would have been irritating. He drifted off into a sleep.

While they were walking up to Chiswick House the next morning Casson scrutinized him closely. Perry looked tired, but not as tired as he had done the day before. He seemed to be recovering balance. Which was all to the good. Every time you were knocked off poise you found it the more difficult to regain.

Chiswick House was a stately and imprisoned grace among lawns. As they walked up the drive between two rows of stone urns and stone figures, the six pillars of the magnificent façade contrasted oddly with the steel scaffolding which caged the still unrestored portion of the house.

The two completed galleries were cool in contrast to the golden warmth outside. Casson and Perry moved slowly through them, remarking on a high-backed, heavily carved chair in dark wood, on a blue-and-brown tapestry of a hunting scene, admiring a crystal and silver reliquary casket. Perry gloated over the casket, his eyes fixed unblinkingly on it, his hands tightly clenched by his sides, his shoulders stiff.

'Marvellous,' said Perry, staring at the bright box. 'Marvellous. Think of all the people kneeling before it. Think of them adoring it. Think of that. And they weren't allowed to touch it!'

There was something obscene in this brown-suited man gazing with such desire at a thing which had housed the object of adoration: gazing at it, moreover, not with the mesmerized hatred of the Puritan whose soul hungered to destroy the glittering idol, nor with the humble avarice of the great collector, but with the mean and voracious greed of the man who must possess something which no man else could touch.

When they emerged and walked under the ancient trees towards the gate, the fullness of the summer heat was falling on the morning. They strolled slowly up Burlington Lane. Casson stopped to light a cigarette and, cupping the lighter in his hands, glanced backwards. Behind them were the two plain-clothes men. One of them nodded slightly.

Casson and Perry strolled on. When they turned into Chiswick Lane, the two policemen crossed the road and walked at a brisk pace up the opposite side. Rapidly they over overhauled Casson and Perry, who were merely ambling. Out of the corner of his eye Casson saw them draw level. They looked at one another and crossed the road again.

The taller of the two – Detective Sergeant Villiers, Casson remembered – came straight up to them and addressed Casson.

'Excuse me, sir,' he said. 'I am a police officer.' He held out his worn, shiny wallet to show the warrant-card in its talc-faced holder. 'I wonder if you and this other gentleman would care to help us?'

'I am always delighted to help the Law,' Casson replied pompously. 'What do you wish us to do? Test the rope for an execution?'

A muscle twitched convulsively in Villiers's cheek and his lips shut tight. Apart from these signs his face remained impassive. Casson heard the faint intake of breath from Perry.

'No, sir,' Villiers replied. 'We have an identification parade, and we should be most obliged if you and this gentleman would act as – er – dummies. It's purely voluntary, of course, but it won't take you a minute and you would be helping us.'

'I don't think . . .' Perry began, but Casson broke in on him:

'We shall come with you, Officer,' Casson replied. 'It will be an experience to remember. I shall enjoy it.'

Reluctantly Perry moved off with them. When the police officers had drawn ahead, Perry whispered to Casson:

'I've got to get back for my dinner, you know. You go along without me.'

'I wouldn't dream of it,' Casson replied heartily. 'Come and enjoy yourself, and I'll stand you lunch afterwards.'

'I don't think I will,' Perry mumbled. 'I feel a trifle indisposed, you know. I think I'll go home. It's probably the heat.'

'Don't be a spoil-sport,' Casson said loudly. 'Besides, it's one's duty to help the police, you know.' The other Detective-Sergeant walking in front with Villiers half-turned his head, as if he had overheard what Casson was saying.

Perry was quiet until they had come out into the Chiswick High Road and turned towards the police station. Then he pulled a watch out of his pocket and looked at it.

'I think I really must go home,' he said firmly. 'I've just remembered I left something in the oven.'

'You can't go now, old man,' said Casson. 'They won't believe that old yarn for a moment and they'll think you've got a guilty conscience or something. Come on. There's nothing to it.'

They had only been in the waiting-room of the police station for a minute when Superintendent Weldon came in. Although he and Casson and Strutt had been in conference six days before, he gave no sign of recognition. His entrance cut short Perry's querulous irritation.

Weldon did not glance at Perry. He spoke to Casson.

'Much obliged to you gentlemen,' he said. 'We won't detain you long. If you'd be kind enough to step into the yard and line up with the other men there, it'll be all be over in a minute.'

In the yard of the police station they joined a straggling line of assorted men, one of whom had a red, right-angled scar running down his cheek and along his jaw. There were about a dozen in all: among them two youths with combed, glossy hair and flamboyant ties, and a nondescript man absorbed in his perusal of *Sporting Life*. At the far end of the yard a uniformed constable watched them from the driving-seat of a black, polished police car.

'I say,' Casson whispered to Perry, 'it'd be jolly funny if the identifying chap picked on me, wouldn't it?' He chuckled. 'Especially for bigamy, as I'm not married. Or you for counterfeiting or something. I suppose you aren't a coiner, are you? I've always had a secret yearning to be one. Jolly clever trade. I always think there must be something rather fascinating in making half-crowns.'

Perry swayed and his body brushed Casson's elbow. Casson could feel him trembling. A momentary pity seized him as he recognized how Perry's lonely defences were being battered. Perry was pale and there was a glisten of sweat on his forehead.

'Here, hold up, old chap,' said Casson. 'You look as if you had seen a ghost.'

'I don't feel very well,' Perry muttered. 'I think I must have caught a chill.'

'That'll be all right,' Casson reassured him. 'It's just nerves. I always have a guilty feeling myself whenever I see a copper.'

Perry's mouth was a narrow, shut line, quite bloodless.

Weldon came out of the police offices with a younger man, clean-shaven and fresh-faced, wearing a neat grey suit. Casson did not recognize him but would have wagered a fiver that he was another policeman acting the part for the occasion.

Very slowly the two men walked up the line, Weldon two paces behind the man in the grey suit. The latter scrutinized each face as he passed. There was dead silence as they proceeded, and even Casson, who knew that the whole show was a put-up job for Perry's benefit, felt his heart beating faster. There was something relentless about this unhurried parade of authority.

The two reached the far end of the line. They held a whispered consultation. They came back again. Each face was scrutinized once more. One of the glossy-haired youths shuffled his feet. The man with the newspaper stared belligerently at Weldon. Opposite Perry the grey-suited man paused for a moment longer than he had done before the others. He passed on to Casson, gave him a long look. Casson's right eyelid drooped and the man turned away, shaking his head.

Weldon addressed the line of uncomfortable men.

'Thank you, gentlemen,' he said. 'Much obliged to you, I'm sure. You can go now.'

The two youths straightened their ties and swaggered off. The man with the newspaper took it out of his pocket, made a mark with his thumbnail against the name of a horse, and folded the paper carefully. 'Bloody bogeys,' he said with great scorn and rolled towards the gate of the yard.

Casson took Perry by the arm.

'Well, old chap,' he said cheerfully. 'They didn't get us that time. Come along and I'll buy you a drink.' He steered him towards the police offices, wishing to give him another taste of the grimly efficient interior of a 'nick'.

In the corridor they met Constable Bentley, also laid on for the occasion.

''Morning, Mr Perry,' he said. 'All those antiquities of yours safe and sound, eh? Can't be too careful, you know, sir.'

Perry muttered something and made for the door.

Once in the street he tugged a handkerchief out of his shirtcuff and mopped his face. He took off his spectacles and cleaned them, and the inexpressive, weak eyes gazed into the sunlight. Casson watched him hungrily. He was going all right, was that one. He had begun to run, and once they began they couldn't stop. Well, let him run until the fatigue in his body caught up with the terror in his mind and both collapsed.

'Come and have a drink,' said Casson. 'You look as if you need it.'

A hundred yards down the High Street they went into a public-house.

'What'll you have?' Casson asked.

'I think a whisky, thank you,' Perry replied. 'I feel rather poorly.'

He drank his double whisky in three gulps, breathing hard. As the spirits sank, he seemed to feel better. Such colour as there ever was in his cheeks returned to them. Only his hand, where it rested the glass on the bar counter, still trembled. Casson ordered two more doubles, and Perry made no attempt to stop him. He took his second drink more slowly, and Casson could watch the confidence returning. Gradually he straightened himself up. He uttered that strangled and humourless laugh.

'It was those unpleasant persons in the courtyard of the police station,' he said. 'They made me feel queer. They looked so common.'

Casson agreed, marvelling at the mind which could produce such a monstrous statement. Then he escorted Perry home, for the little man was becoming unsteady on his feet. For a moment Casson toyed with the idea of insisting on going into Perry's house with him and trying to break him then and there. Regretfully, he decided that Perry was not yet sufficiently scared for mere alcohol to break down his reserve.

Casson had his lunch and went up to Savile Row.

'Well,' said Strutt, 'how's he cooking?'

'Nicely. The show this morning upset him quite a lot.'

'Is he ripe?'

'We've got a way to go. What about putting the bloodhounds on to him?'

Strutt shut the window. The heat in the small room became stifling but he did not seem to notice it. At length he said:

'You don't think we'll lose him?'

'Why should we?'

'If we have him followed so that he notices, he'll know we're after him. Once he knows that, he'll skip. These boys always do. One fine morning he'll up and skip and be gone without so much as kiss your hand. He'll go to Manchester or Cardiff or Liverpool or somewhere, and we shan't find him for months. It's too risky. We daren't lose him.'

'Frightened of your promotion?' Casson teased.

Strutt kicked his waste-paper basket across the room. Casson laughed.

'They always rise,' he commented. 'Like great, fat salmon, they rise. Delightful.' Strutt grinned.

'But he'll slip us, you know.'

'He won't,' Casson said. 'For three reasons. In the first place, he won't go without his precious museum. It's the only love – or rather the only background – which he has to his life, and he'll have to take it with him. That means he'll have to have a furniture van, and so we shall know if he's going and where he goes. In the second place, he couldn't live now by any other trade except blackmail. It will take him too long to find new victims in Manchester or Cardiff or Blackpool or wherever it is. Furthermore, he must have some milch-cows left here in London. He will have known from his time in the Bank which customers were liable for the squeeze, and he will merely have kept himself up-to-date by using Macfarlane. He'll milk his remaining victims before he thinks of cutting loose from London. . . .'

'He'll go to Japan, and we can't have him extradited.'

'He can't speak a foreign language. He told me so. He won't go to a country in which he can't talk. He wouldn't be happy in strange territory. I guarantee he won't skip.'

'All right,' said Strutt. 'I'll put the dogs on him.'

'With the biggest possible boots?'

'With boots like barges.'

'You'll be Commissioner yet.'

'But,' said Strutt, 'I'll give you no more than a week. Understand?'

'No,' Casson replied and reached for his gloves.

'Give me a cigarette, will you?' Casson looked up, surprised.

'I thought you didn't smoke cigarettes?'

'I don't. I've given them up. I can't afford them. But now I feel like a girl going out to her first party.'

Casson gave him one and Strutt smoked it in savage puffs for a third of its length. He threw it down on the floor and ground it out.

'Horrible,' he said. 'Good-bye.'

Casson shut the door behind him and walked down the bare

corridor, then he went back and put his head round the door. Strutt was still grinding out the remains of the cigarette on the floor.

'Is the girl still employed by those lawyers in Essex Street?' he asked.

'Shaw? Yes.'

'Thanks.' Casson went away. He put in three hours' work at his office and returned to Hammersmith.

Perry did not appear in the Shepley Arms that evening but the candles were lit in his first-floor museum, and they were not snuffed out until after midnight.

Perry had been sitting quite still, watching them. He sat in one of the high-backed wing chairs, fighting a battle against panic. He had not experienced this sort of creeping hysteria, not, at any rate, since he was first sent to school. He repeated to himself aphorisms from Marcus Aurelius but they made no comforting vibration on the nerves. He fell back on logic. He could not have gone wrong, he assured himself. There were only two points on which he could possibly have erred, and on those his memory checked that he had done what he had intended to do. On those points he was sure of his memory – as sure as memory could be.

He swallowed two more aspirins that night, excusing his lapse by telling himself that he really had caught a chill and would feel better when he had sweated it out. He wished he had some whisky in the house.

For the whole of the next day Casson watched No. 51. His own ordinary life had dropped into an irrelevant background. The pleasant office in Vigo Street, his comfortable flat, the good wine at Cane's, his friends, his pictures, his plans: they had all been submerged under the pattern into which Perry had drawn him. That pattern was becoming stiff, rigid, and inexorable, drawn taut. His own nerves were beginning to respond, strung as tight as the pattern itself.

At six Perry set off towards the Shepley Arms. Casson followed and joined him in their corner of the saloon bar. Casson drank half his pint straight off and watched Perry over the rim of his tankard. The little man looked seedy, pouched under the eyes. He was carelessly shaved. He had drunk half a double whisky.

157

'You look rotten,' said Casson. 'You ought to take a tonic.'

Perry's glance slithered towards him and quickly away again.

'It's that chill,' he replied. 'That's why I had a whisky this evening.'

'Run down,' Casson observed. 'What you want is a couple of days by the sea.' He saw Perry stiffen, and knew that in both of their minds was the memory of that last journey to Brighton which Perry had made before the death of Macfarlane.

'I'm all right, really,' Perry said, and finished his whisky.

'I'll get you another.' Casson rose and took the empty glass and his own tankard. Perry made no gesture of protest. Casson brought the drinks back.

'Why don't you go to Brighton?' he suggested, as he sat down again. Perry looked at him.

'Brighton? I don't like it.'

'Wonderful place. Those Regency houses. And the air's like wine. It's a bit crowded, of course. When were you last there?'

For a second Perry hesitated.

'Years ago,' he replied. Excellent, thought Casson. He has begun to lie. He must be cracking or he wouldn't lie. And once you start lying you can't stop.

'Of course,' Casson continued, 'if you don't like Brighton, you ought to go to Dover. It's a queer place because there you can be absolutely alone. Those huge white cliffs looking down on you and everybody else busy travelling in and out across the Channel leave you marooned as though you were on a desert island. It's a place people use like a turnstile between London and Paris, so they never bother you if you are just sitting there. They pass you by. Even in the Lord Warden Hotel you feel alone because everyone else is thinking about passports.'

Perry made no comment. He continued to sip his whisky and stare at his shoes. Suddenly he finished his drink, muttered good night, and went.

Casson was at his window early next morning. There were Strutt's bloodhounds, ostentatiously and obviously policemen in plain clothes, both reading newspapers, one at each end of the street. As they had been instructed, they made no attempt at concealment.

Perry appeared with his black shopping bag. Slowly, deliberately, one of the policemen folded up his paper and followed. Peering obliquely up the street Casson saw the second constable give Perry a hard stare as the little man passed him. He too folded up his newspaper and followed. The three went out of sight.

Perry returned an hour later, walking fast, still followed. The two policemen settled down once more to their papers. They took it in turns to have lunch. They remained in Bickersteth Street all the afternoon, lounging in whatever shade they could find. They followed Perry to the Shepley Arms. One of them came into the pub and slowly consumed half-a-pint until Perry left again.

The same thing happened next day with two different policemen. When Casson entered the Shepley Arms that evening, he saw Perry in his habitual corner, a half-pint before him on the table, his head in his hands, staring down at the floor. He started as Casson put down his own pint.

'I say,' Casson exclaimed, 'you do look wretched, old chap. You ought to see a doctor.'

Perry's skin was a queer, unhealthy colour. Now and again one of his eyelids twitched.

'It's nothing,' he replied.

'Well, you ought to take a pull,' Casson persisted. 'You'll be having a nervous breakdown next.'

Perry sat up.

'What makes you say that?'

'You look so odd – almost like those chaps who think they're being persecuted. I've met one or two of them. Very odd characters.'

'Para—' Perry could not pronounce the word.

'Paranoiacs. That's right.'

'How do they – how do they go like that?'

'Oh, they lose a bit of control and then they're away.'

'Lose control?'

'Their nerves get out of hand. But the cure can be quite easy – that's to say with the stronger ones.'

'Yes?' Perry leant forward.

'Take them out of their environment. Put them somewhere where they've never been before, somewhere where they can relax for a time. They get back a bit of poise and, if they're tough enough, they get back their full control. At least, that's what I've always thought.'

'I see. Yes.' Casson chattered about other things but Perry scarcely seemed to listen. Once he interrupted to ask: 'What was that place you told me about at Dover?' and, when Casson had told him, he fell silent again. At length he said: 'Well, I must be going. I promised myself I would have an early bed.'

The candles did not burn in the front room of No. 51 that night, and Perry went out at his usual time the next morning. But he carried no shopping bag and, although the day was as cloudlessly fine as those which had gone before, he had a mackintosh over his arm. Casson noted this and grinned wickedly to himself. He hoped and believed that Perry would evade his two followers.

An hour later a fat figure swung ponderously down the street. Strutt's eyes were bulging and he looked very angry. Casson heard the sound of a short conversation downstairs and then the Superintendent burst into the room. Carefully he shut the door.

'You ruddy amateur. . . .'

'Tush,' Casson replied. 'Temper. Temper. What's eating you?'

'He's gone, skipped, ruddy well bunked. May you burn. You've lost him. I knew it would happen. Bungled. . . .'

'Your boys lost him?'

'Curse them. He did the old trick. Waited in a street until there was only one taxi in sight and then hailed it. Told it to go to Charing Cross. Fortunately it was a radio taxi and we got on to the owners and had it driven straight to the nick. Ruddy useless. Perry had told the driver he'd changed his mind and wanted to be dropped at Sloane Square. So he was. So there.'

'Fine,' said Casson.

'Fine!' Strutt's face went redder.

'Have you got a car here?' Casson asked.

'Do you think I rode a burning horse?'

'Then you can drive me to my garage.' He consulted his watch. 'Plenty of time.'

'Time for what? More of your brilliant plots?'

'Time to see John Perry.'

'You know where he is?'

'Yes.'

'Where?'

'I'll tell you this evening.'

'It may be too late.'

'It won't be.'

Strutt stamped in anger.

'What the hell's happening?' he demanded.

'The last lap,' Casson replied. 'Come on.'

Chapter Fourteen

CASSON got out the Rolls and drove down to the offices of Liggett and Benson in Essex Street where Jean Shaw worked. He had a brief interview with one of the partners, and she was brought to him in the waiting-room.

'Good morning,' she said, still antagonistic.

'I have asked if you could have the rest of the day off. I would be very grateful if you would come with me.'

She looked startled.

'What's happened?'

'We think that, at last, we are going to get the man who murdered your Jim.'

'You're going to arrest him?'

'At the moment we can't arrest him.'

'Then . . . ?'

'That is where I think you can help.'

'Me? How?'

'I want you to meet him.' Her face went white.

'But I couldn't. Oh, no. Please.' Her habitual self-control had left her.

'I promise you, Miss Shaw, that it is the only way.' Automatically she tidied the copies of the *Guardian* on the round table.

'Do you mean that you want him to try to murder me so that you can catch him in the act?' Her voice was hostile.

Casson smiled.

'No,' he replied gently. 'I wouldn't let him try that. In any case he wouldn't do it.' He picked up his gloves. 'Will you trust me, Miss Shaw?'

She hesitated.

'Very well. I must get my bag.'

As she climbed into the Rolls and he shut the door behind her, he noticed the faces of secretaries peering at them from an open upper window. He smiled to himself. What stories they would invent about her being driven away in a Rolls! And how desperately wrong they would be! Not even he, if he had been a casual bystander watching that scene, could have imagined that a young girl was being driven to meet the murderer of her fiancé.

They drove in silence across Vauxhall Bridge, through Lewisham, and along the Sidcup Bypass towards Wrotham. Casson drove fast and, although he might have seemed dangerous, he knew and loved his car so well that he had supreme self-confidence. Jean Shaw did not. She sat stiffly in her seat, her hands gripped together. At last she said:

'I am sorry, Mr Duker, but I am not used to motor cars. Could you drive a little slower?' Casson looked at the clock on the dashboard, made a swift calculation, and dropped speed. She did not speak again until they were past Wrotham and approaching West Malling.

'Where are you taking me?' she asked.

'Dover.'

'Why Dover?' Her question was matter of fact.

'That's where Perry is.' Casson hoped that he was there. He had no desire either to look a fool or to lose the blackmailer.

'I don't like it,' she said.

'Nor do I,' he replied. 'But Mr Perry is not thinking of our convenience.' There was another long silence.

'I would be glad if you would put me down,' she said at last. 'I can get a train home.'

'You will be quite safe,' he retorted. He glanced at her and saw by the flush in her face that he had hit a mark.

'I am not worried about my safety, Mr Duker. I just do not like this business and I do not see what good I can do. I should be glad if you would put me down.'

He slithered the huge car to a stop, braking so hard that she had to hold on to the dashboard. He leaned across and opened the door.

'Get out, child,' he said. 'Get out and go home. And when Perry kills his next one we'll send you a postcard.'

In silence she shut the door and they drove on. He tried to lessen the coldness between them by making conversation but it was of no use. He let his mind return to his calculations about

Perry's movements. He would not go to Brighton, not again, not after his last visit there before the murder of Macfarlane. Brighton would be contaminated for him. He would not be able to think there in peace. Memories of his crimes, particularly of the murder, would crowd in upon him and disturb him. Casson had planted the seed of Dover in his mind, and to Dover he would go. It was uncontaminated. There he would be able to think; or so he would reckon. There he would be able to recover from his panic: or so he would hope.

When they reached the Port, Casson left her in the car while he searched the Lord Warden for his quarry. There was no sign of Perry in any of the lounges. An inquiry at the reception desk told him that the hotel was full and that all the bookings had been made over a week before. He went out into the glass-fronted lounge which faced the sea.

The beach was almost deserted. There was no sign of Perry. Was he having a meal in one of the many small cafés in the town? Then a woman sitting on the beach, adjusting the scarf round her head, lay back, and he saw Perry.

The little man was sitting on his mackintosh, his arms clasped round his legs, staring out to sea. By his side on the raincoat was a package wrapped up in white paper. He looked like a brown smudge, shapelessly hunched on the long, curved bar of bright sand. He might have been a pile of flotsam waiting for the vivid blue sea to come and wash him away.

Casson collected Jean Shaw and took her into the glass lounge. He pointed down the beach to where Perry was sitting on his mackintosh.

'You see that man? The one next to a woman in a red bathing-dress?'

'The one in a brown suit?'

'Yes. That's the man who murdered Jim.' He lit a cigarette and turned to order coffee. When he turned back again, she was standing there, motionless, staring.

'It's impossible,' she breathed. 'He looks so insignificant.'

'That's why he succeeded.'

She gripped his arm.

'Look! He's eating sandwiches.' Perry had dipped his hand into the white paper package and taken out a round of bread. He sat gazing out to sea, chewing.

'Even murderers must eat,' he commented. She did not seem to have heard him.

'But it's so – it's so incongruous.'

'Have some coffee.' He poured it out for her and added milk and sugar. He adjusted his chair so that he could watch Perry without having to get up. Jean Shaw stood by the window, staring down at the beach.

'Have your coffee,' he reminded her.

She sat down.

'What is he doing?' she asked.

Casson smiled.

'He is trying to think clearly. He is trying to remember if he made a mistake.'

'Did he?'

'No.'

'Then why is he worrying?'

'He knows we are after him. He does not understand how we have found him. He feels he is putting his head into a trap. He does not understand how there can be a trap. He is having a very unpleasant afternoon. Especially since he can't make up his mind whether there is a way of escape.'

'Is there?' The Scots plaint in her voice softened the harshness of her question.

'There are two. He can assume another identity and hide. He won't do that because he will feel that he is always being hunted and he will have to abandon his loot. The other way is for him to go back to London, resume his normal life, and face out whatever is coming to him. That is the safe and that is the foolproof way. But he does not know it's foolproof because he does not know if he has made a mistake. And if he did make a mistake, he will hang.'

'What will he do?'

'Go back to London and face it out. There is nothing else that a man of his psychology could do.'

'But – but why are we here, then?'

'In an hour or so he will have made up his mind to return. He will have restored some sort of confidence in himself. When he feels better, he will meet us together – as it were by accident he will meet us – and his new-found armour will be splintered at a stroke. I am the only friend he has got – or so he thinks. He does not know that I know you. In the one place which he has chosen as a haven of solitude, he meets me with the fiancée of the man he murdered. I defy any criminal to be proof against that.'

She shivered.

'I think it's beastly,' she said, looking away.

He did not bother to reply. He watched Perry. Jean Shaw took up a magazine and flipped over the pages: put it down again. For a time she observed him. He could feel her gaze but he never moved. He watched Perry. The yachts in the harbour bobbed up and down, their green-and-white hulls making a juggling pattern against the far wall of the harbour. The Townshend ferry slid out to sea with its load of holiday cars. All the time, for a long time, he watched Perry.

At last the little man got to his feet, brushed the sand from his trousers, and gathered up his mackintosh. He stumbled up the beach, his shoes slipping in the sand.

'Come along,' said Casson. 'This is it.' She followed him through the hall and out of the hotel. As they went he said to her:

'When you meet him, don't say anything unusual.' He took her arm for an instant. 'Bear up, Jean. We really do need you.'

They stood behind a parked charabanc and watched him come round the corner of the hotel. He entered the Lord Warden. Casson gave him ten minutes. Then he and the girl followed.

Perry was sitting in a far corner of the lounge. He did not look round as they came in. Casson arranged the girl so that she sat with her back to Perry. He ordered tea. When she had poured out for them both, he took a piece of bread-and-butter and leant back, twisting in his chair so that he could see the blackmailer. Perry was staring out of the window.

'Good heavens!' said Casson, in a loud voice. 'There's a friend of mine.' He rose to his feet and strolled over.

Perry was putting down his cup as Casson approached. He glanced up and saw Casson. His mouth sagged open. The remainder of his tea slopped into the saucer.

'Hullo,' Casson said heartily. 'What are you doing here, you old dog?'

Perry continued to stare at him.

'You must come and meet a friend of mine,' Casson continued. 'Fancy meeting you here! Come and join us.'

Perry appeared to collect himself.

'Thank you,' he said thickly. 'Thank you. I won't, thank you very much. I've got to catch a train back to London.' He drew a deep breath. 'I came down for the day, you know, to get some sea air. As you advised me.'

Casson had his hand on his arm and almost hauled him to his feet.

'Come on,' he chuckled. 'You sly dog.' Perry tried to refuse but he was hustled over to Casson's table. As they neared it, he felt Perry's body go rigid.

'Here we are,' said Casson. 'Let me introduce you. Mr John Perry – Miss Jean Shaw.'

'How do you do,' she said, her voice steady. How indeed? thought Casson. He pushed Perry into a chair and waved to the waiter to bring another cup.

'Jolly nice place this,' he rattled on. 'All those boats going to France and Belgium. Makes me want to get away from it all. What about you, Jean?'

'I prefer this country. In England you know exactly where you are. Don't you?' she replied in the same even voice. At last Casson dared to look at her. Her face was pale but composed. She was entirely under control except for the shivering of muscles in the back of her hand. If he had prompted her himself she could not have made a better reply.

He glanced at Perry. Perry was leaning back in his chair, scarcely breathing. He had gone a sallow, sick colour. After a moment he clawed at the arm of his chair and forced himself to his feet.

'I beg your pardon,' he muttered. 'It must be the sun. If you'll excuse me.'

Casson leapt to his feet.

'My dear chap, you're ill. You wait here, Jean. I'll take Mr Perry out for a breath of air.'

'No, thank you,' said Perry. 'No, thank you. Excuse me. I

really must go.' He almost forced Casson's hand from his arm and walked unsteadily out of the room. Casson sat down.

'I am sorry,' he said to her. 'And I am very grateful.' Her eyes were shut. 'Take it easy,' he urged. He hoped to God that she was not going to faint. Slowly she opened her eyes.

'I have been defiled,' she said in a matter-of-fact voice. The Biblical ring of the phrase, the word she must have remembered from youthful Sundays in a Lowland kirk, struck him to the heart. He signalled to the waiter.

'Bring coffee. Bring it quick.'

When it came he poured brandy into it from a pocket flask and gave it to her.

'Drink this, my dear,' he said. 'Please.' She took a mouthful of it, coughed, put the cup down on the table.

'Finish it,' he ordered her. She shook her head.

'Finish it, Jean.' She finished it.

'Now can we go?' she asked.

'Yes. It is all over – for you – for the moment.'

They drove back in silence. In Maidstone Casson said: 'I hope you will accept my apology. I assure you that today was necessary,' but she made no answer. He dropped her at her lodgings in Disraeli Road and went back to his flat.

'What's the matter, sir?' asked Mrs Baker when she saw him. Had the strain told that much, he wondered, and looked at himself in the hall mirror. If you were romantically minded you might have said that the lean face looked haunted but he was not romantically minded and he would not even admit that it looked tired.

'Would you get me one of those half-bottles of non-vintage Bollinger?' he said to her. 'Pour it all out into a large glass and put some brandy in it.'

He picked up the telephone and dialled the number for West End Central. He asked for Strutt. When the heavy voice came on the line he said:

'He's back in Chiswick. He's ripe. You can pick him up this evening. I'm going out there now. If he doesn't come out of his house by ten, you'd better go in and get him.'

Strutt's voice boomed back at him:

'Will he break?'

'I think so.'

There was a long pause. Then Strutt said:

'Good luck, boy. If we don't bust him tonight he'll never hang.'

Chapter Fifteen

CASSON took a taxi straight to the Shepley Arms. Peter the barman told him that Mr Perry had not been in that evening. Indeed, Casson hardly expected that he would have had the desire for beer. His only and desperate need, after the mental beating which he had received that afternoon, would be to hide: to hide and rest: to rest and recover.

Casson went back to Mrs Gunn's. He sat by the window in his bedroom, chain smoking. His mind moved in hot, narrow orbits of impatience. In a spasm of lucidity he recognized that the chase exacted its price from the hunters as well as from the hunted.

The two plain-clothes policemen were at their stations in the street. If Perry had returned home he would be caged. But if he had not gone back to London that afternoon he might be anywhere between Bristol and Bradford, a prim and desperate man whose dream of beauty had been wrenched from him: a man who, in the double rage of failure and deprivation, would take any revenge that lay within the span of his cowardice. And if he had gone on the run, then Casson had lost him: lost him at the crucial moment of the whole operation when Perry's mind should have been worn ragged with uncertainty.

Casson emptied the ashtray and stared into Bickersteth Street. The dusty leaves of the lilac up the road were sharply motionless. No curtain moved in the open windows. The diffused gold of a London summer evening lay between the houses, but tonight it was not mellow; it was merely the suspended illumination of heat. There were no chinks or corridors in that heat through which a wind could blow and move the leaves of the lilac.

Casson washed his hands and face and returned to his seat in the window. An old Scots terrier waddled up the pavement, checking each lamp-post. A woman came out and called him home – 'Mac! Mac!' she called. A taxi rattled down the street and turned the corner by Perry's house. One of the policemen in the street coughed with the gasping irritation of smoker's throat.

He took a fresh cigarette and threw away the crumpled packet.

Then Perry came out.

I wonder why, thought Casson. I wonder why. Could he no longer bear the weight of his thoughts? Had he been driven out by them, like Orestes pursued by the Furies after his mother's murder? Had he been driven by them from his silent rooms into the open air, driven out to try and muffle the beat of those iron and harrying wings by the noises of people in King Street, Hammersmith?

The watching policeman in Perry's rear made a signal with his hand. Casson leaned forward.

A black Wolseley car began to crawl down the street. As it approached Perry, it slewed over to his side of the road. It jerked to an abrupt stop by the kerb and two plain-clothes men got out of the back.

They spoke to Perry. Perry shook his head violently and made as if to go on. One of the officers laid his hand on the little man's arm. Perry stopped. The officer nodded his head towards the car. Perry looked back down the street towards his own house, then at the car, then back down the street. He stumbled into the car.

The doors slammed and it skidded away from the kerb, accelerating rapidly down the street. The arrest could not have lasted more than a minute. It had been swift, discreet, and irresistibly efficient. Its psychological effect on the victim should have been considerable.

Casson filled his cigarette-case, picked up a thin, bound volume and walked leisurely through the airless dusk to the Chiswick Police Station. He was no longer impatient.

In the station hall he met P.C. Bentley. The young constable was in mufti, wearing a smart green tweed coat and grey flannel trousers.

'Evening, sir.'

'Evening, Bentley,' Casson replied. 'Good show of yours the other night. Is the Superintendent in?'

'This way, sir.' He led on. There seemed to be a lot of policemen in the station – more than there should be for that time of night.

'By the way,' said Casson, 'what are you doing here in mufti? Have they put you into the C.I.D.?'

Bentley laughed a happy, healthy laugh.

'No, sir. I came in to see the fun. My first murder case, sir. I'd like to see him get the bullet.'

Casson understood why the other policemen were hanging about in whispering groups.

Superintendent Weldon was leaning against the brown-painted mantelpiece of his office, drinking a cup of tea. He nodded to Casson.

'Strutt's with him.'

'What's he doing?'

The grizzled man by the fireplace grinned, disclosing a gleaming set of dentures.

'Talking to him like an uncle. I wish I could get my hands on him,' he added, putting down his cup with a bang on the desk.

'What's he look like?'

'The basket he is.'

Casson gave up the conversation. He smoked half a cigarette before Strutt entered. Strutt ran his forefinger round his neck inside his collar-band and sank into Weldon's chair. He undid his waistcoat and relaxed. He and Casson looked at each other in silence, each knowing what lay in the balance, each knowing how delicate and imponderable were the calculations which had brought them to that moment.

'Your turn,' said Strutt.

'How is he?'

'Scared stiff. But sullen. Spouting about his rights. Moaning for a lawyer.' Strutt leered. 'When I asked him the name of his ruddy lawyer and he couldn't think of one, I thought he was going to blub.'

'How long have we got him?'

'Till tomorrow.'

'How did you pick him up? Not on a warrant for murder?'

Strutt was playing with the teaspoon which he had taken from Weldon's saucer.

'We pulled him in under the "Breathing Act",' he said casually.

'What?'

'You know. Loitering with intent. Being a suspicious person. For ruddy well being there at all.'

'And he goes tomorrow?'

'We can't hold him longer.'

'I see.' Strutt had bent the teaspoon double in his fingers while he was talking. He threw it in the waste-paper basket and leaned forward.

'See here, Cass. If we don't get a confession by tomorrow morning we've had it. By then he'll know the strength of our hand. He'll know we're bluffing. He'll know we can never pin it on him. He'll leave here a free and happy man, the little swine.'

'Shall I go to him now?'

'As you wish.'

Without comment Weldon watched them go. The whispered conversations of policemen in the hall died down and heads turned to watch them as they passed.

Strutt nodded to the constable leaning against the door of a cell. He unlocked. Casson walked in. The door slammed behind him.

Perry stared at him in amazement. Colour flooded into his face. His eyes lit up. Then the colour ebbed and the line of the mouth sagged. The eyes went dull.

'What are you doing here?' he said, looking away. Casson sat down on the other of the two chairs.

'I saw them arrest you and I came to see what had happened. What have you done?'

'You came to help?' He turned eagerly.

'Yes. What's the matter?'

'You came to help. That's good. You came to help. You must get me a lawyer. That's what I need. Policemen are afraid of lawyers. He must get me out of here.'

'But what are you in for?'

'I don't know. Two policemen jumped out of a car and asked me if I was a man called John Bellamon or some name like that. When I said I wasn't, they said I'd have to prove it and I'd better go along to the police station with them.'

'But what was this Bellamon bloke wanted for?'

'Burglary. They asked me all sorts of questions about my

173

collection. How did I get it? Where did I get the money? They told me I needn't answer the questions if I didn't want to. And they always came back to the point about where I got the money.'

Casson lit a cigarette.

'Where did you?'

Perry had been looking down at his hands. His head jerked up. 'What?'

'Where did you get the money?'

There was a long pause while Perry stared at him and Casson met his eyes. Perry looked away.

'I told you. I have some private means.'

'Oh, yes. Of course. So you did.' He smoked on for a minute or two in silence. Perry glanced at him several times, then quickly away again. 'I've always thought it an admirable joke,' Casson went on, 'for a humble employee of a bank to extract a thousand pounds from one of his Directors.'

Perry's face had gone ashen.

'What do you mean?'

'What I call the Bagot trick. Remarkably clever.'

'I don't understand you.'

Casson sighed.

'It will come,' he said. 'Have a cigarette?' Perry did not seem to have heard. He was staring fixedly at Casson.

'Are you a policeman?' he asked and his voice sounded as though it were being twisted in his throat.

'Lord, no,' Casson replied.

'But you are a journalist? Like you told me?'

'Yes. To some extent. Yes. I suppose you could call me a journalist.'

'Then you came here for a story?'

'Understanding dawns,' Casson said in a sleepy voice and lit another cigarette. 'I did come here for a story. I came for your story, John Perry.'

'My – my story? I haven't got one.'

'Shall we say, then, that I came for the story of Mr Bagot?'

'Bagot?'

'I must apologize. I should have told you earlier in our acquaintanceship that I knew Lockyer.'

Perry rose to his feet and began walking up and down the cell. Casson let him walk for nearly a minute. Then he yawned and said:

'Do stop it, my dear chap. You sound like a prisoner in the condemned cell.' Perry stopped abruptly, facing the door. Then he swung round, his undistinguished face suddenly made individual by a look of ferocity.

'Get out of here,' he muttered. 'I don't understand a word you're saying. You're mad. Go away.'

Casson gazed at him.

'Do sit down,' he said. 'You'll find it more restful. I'll tell you a tale.'

'Go away,' Perry repeated. 'Go away.'

'It's about you,' said Casson. 'Do you realize why you are here?'

'Of course I do. Of course I do. Those stupid men arrested me on suspicion of being a burglar. But they can't keep me here. They can't. They'll have to let me out in an hour and I'll sue them. It's wrongful arrest.'

'You'll be here longer than an hour.'

'I won't. They can't do it.'

'Perhaps I had better explain,' said Casson patiently. 'You are not really here on suspicion. You are here on a charge of murder.'

Perry was leaning up against the wall, the palms of his hands flat against its white surface. He said nothing. He did not even blink.

'Murder?'

'That's right.'

'Murder,' Perry repeated.

'Yes. Premeditated killing. Murder.'

'Murder,' he repeated. Suddenly he leapt from his position against the bare wall as if he had been a rubber ball bounced off it. He stood in front of Casson and pointed at him.

'You're trying to get a false confession out of me. You're trying to trap me,' he accused.

Casson stubbed out his cigarette.

'I don't have to try,' he observed. 'You are trapped already.'

Perry clenched his fists.

'Who are you?' he demanded, a touch of hysteria in his voice. 'Who are you? What have you got to do with me? Tell me that?'

'I'll tell you a lot more,' said Casson. 'You'd better sit down.' Perry sat on the edge of the bed.

'Let us begin with Mr Greenhaugh and Miss Martin of Hatfield,' he said. 'And then we can go on to Lockyer. Now, when you were a clerk in Gamman's Bank – and, let us face it, not a very good clerk – you went through the accounts of the bank's clients. You went through them with great deliberation. You went through them with a view to ultimate blackmail. When you had obtained enough information about your prospective victims, about their circumstances and their characters, you left the bank. You started to blackmail. One of your first victims was Greenhaugh. You had learnt about Miss Martin. For some days – for nearly a week, in fact – you followed her – as you did, in a different fashion, with Mrs Gordonstoun. You were clever in your disguise: very clever. . . .'

A glint came momentarily into Perry's eyes. Casson noted it, but went on, without a break, in the same tone of voice. He told Perry the whole story as he himself knew it, from Greenhaugh, through Lockyer and Mrs Gordonstoun, to Macfarlane. Once, when he was describing Lockyer's reactions to being blackmailed, he made Perry laugh. It was not a pleasant laugh, but Casson noted that also as another successful twist of the screw.

He glanced at his wrist-watch as he finished his recital. It had taken twenty-seven minutes. At the end of it Perry sat on the edge of the bed, his hands on his knees – exactly as he had been when Casson began.

'Well,' he said, and his voice sounded satisfied, 'it is a very pretty story, but what has it got to do with me? You tell me about a Mr Martin and a Mr Bagot and another person – whatever his name is – '

'Fenton.'

'– and they appear to have blackmailed three people. You presume that the criminal is the same person. Why, I do not know. You seem to presume that the blackmailer is me. Again I do not understand why. It's kind of you to come and see me but I am more concerned with getting out of here and going home than with listening to stories of crime.'

'Are you?' said Casson. He got up and went over to the door.

'Good night,' said Perry. Casson did not answer. He tapped on the door and the constable opened it, let him out and locked it behind him. Casson went into Weldon's office. The two C.I.D. Sergeants who had invited himself and Perry to the mock identity parade were there also. They all looked up as he came in.

Strutt leaned forward, his neck bulging over his collar.

'Has he signed?'

'Nowhere near it. He thinks he is winning. I shall need those photographs I took of him. And a copy of my statement with the dates and times.'

Strutt shoved a flat envelope over the desk to him. Casson chose the photographs he wanted.

'Will he buckle?' Strutt growled.

Casson nodded at him.

'He'll bend. He's got the conceit.'

Strutt flopped back in his chair.

'Good boy. They're all vain. Sex and greed and vanity. That's all there is to crime. Binge the swine up. I don't care if I lick his boots as long as I hang him.'

Casson looked back from the door and addressed Strutt. 'It would be a good thing if you came in. Ten minutes' time. Say something terse. Then retire. It makes a change.'

Casson went back to the cell. Perry was sitting on the other chair, his arms crossed. He was gazing up at the ceiling.

Casson threw the photographs on the bed. They were the enlargements of Perry as himself and as Bagot.

'Have a look at those,' he said. When Perry had looked through them, he replaced them in a neat pile on the bed and refolded his arms.

'I have identified you as John Perry and Mr Bagot,' Casson said. 'Miss Martin, Henry Lockyer, and Mrs Gordonstoun have identified those photographs of you disguised as Martin, as Bagot – and as Fenton.' Perry said nothing.

Casson unfolded the typed copy of his statement.

'Here is the chronicle.' He read out the dates and times of the places in which Perry had been ever since Casson had started his watch from Bickersteth Street. At the end of the recital Perry shifted uneasily on his chair. He was about to say something but Casson did not let him. He pulled a small notebook out of his pocket.

'Here is some more.' He related Perry's following of Jean Shaw and his persuasive evenings in pubs with Macfarlane during the week before Macfarlane's death. When he had finished, a silence fell between them. Casson lit a cigarette and waited.

'I knew young Macfarlane,' said Perry in a normal voice. 'He was quite a nice person.'

'A pity you felt that you had to kill him. It was unnecessary, you know.' Perry's lips tightened.

'I understand that the poor young man committed suicide.'

'You told him that his fiancée was a wanton – that was the word you used, wasn't it? – and you knew he'd fall for that story and that she'd be unable to prove that she wasn't. You recommended him to take a sleeping draught because he was so worried. You made him rather drunk in that pub on the night you killed him. You took him back to his flat and gave him the last dose of chloral. You turned on the gas, pulled the rug against the door from the outside, and went home. But you were a bit tipsy yourself that night. You had had more than you were accustomed to. You had planned the crime when you were sober. But it is always possible to overlook some detail when you are tipsy.'

Perry was looking at him unblinking.

'What do you mean?' His voice was not steady.

At that moment the door was unlocked and thrown open. Strutt thrust his head in and glared at Perry. Of Casson he took no notice.

'What time do you wake up?' he asked Perry. Perry gaped at him.

'Half past seven,' he replied.

'Good,' said Strutt. 'When they come to fetch you, you won't have to be woken. They always hang them at nine.' The door slammed shut again.

Perry was breathing heavily.

'It's intimidation,' he said hoarsely. He turned to Casson.

'You have been spying on me. You've framed me. You have.'

'Since you bought those statuettes I have been spying on you,' Casson replied. 'From what Henry Lockyer told me I imagined the sort of person you were. I knew that in the end I should find you. I did so. I found you at Christie's. Since that afternoon I followed you day and night. I took photographs of you with a telephoto camera. I watched you through high-power binoculars and I learnt to know your facial expressions. You have been living under an invisible searchlight. You have been wriggling like a worm under a microscope. I have analysed your mind, calculated your motives, tabulated your reactions. I know what you drink, what your past is, what you dream about. It has been a fascinating study.'

Perry's hands were shaking.

'You devil,' he whispered.

'Not only,' Casson went on, unmoved, 'do I know everything about your past: I know everything about your future.'

'My future? How can you?'

'You are going to hang.'

Perry gripped his hands between his knees as though to stop them shaking. He stared at Casson.

'No,' he breathed. 'No. No, I'm not.'

Casson shrugged.

'There's no evidence,' Perry went on.

Casson looked at him coldly.

'That's your view.'

'There isn't.' His body was trembling.

Casson got up and walked over to the door of the cell.

'Wait a minute,' said Perry. 'I want to know one thing. Why are you here?'

Casson turned round and scrutinized him. Perry's face was grey. He seemed to have difficulty in swallowing.

'I came to save you from oblivion,' said Casson evenly.

'What's that mean? To save me? I knew you would.'

'Not to save you from the gallows: from oblivion.'

'I don't understand. I've got a headache. It's all that nonsense you've been telling me. You can't believe it. You couldn't.'

Casson sat down. He waited before he spoke again. This was

the moment for which he had so long planned and into it he must concentrate all of his personality.

'It is my view that you will hang,' he began. 'You will be convicted, and that will be that. You will be written up in the newspapers as a despicable murderer. I doubt whether your story will make the headlines. Even if it does no one will remember you after you are cut down in the execution shed.

'Now, I have studied you for a long time. I have studied you closely. I believe that I understand you better than anyone else has ever done.' Perry had his head between his hands and his elbows resting on his knees. He was looking down at the floor. 'You see,' Casson continued, 'I also love things of beauty. We are both connoisseurs. It is for this reason that I, and I alone, do not think of you as a common criminal. You are unusual, peculiar, unique.' Perry glanced up for a second, then turned his gaze back to the floor. 'You are a man of humble beginnings who had ambition. It was an unusual ambition. You chose unusual means to get it. You did get it. You waited and plotted and blackmailed so that you could create a private and sacrosanct world, a small, safe, and glowing universe. I condemn the means you used but I am forced to admit that there is a kind of twisted poetry in your career.

'You are going to hang. If I write your story after you are dead you will become a legend. Instead of being a statistic in the year's crime record, you will go into history as an individual, as an eccentric, as an exotic flower which fed its appetites on fears. You will be known as the man who murdered in order to retain two Queen Anne chairs, two Georgian candlesticks, six blue Bristol glasses, and a harewood secretaire. That is your legend, and I alone can write it.'

He paused. Perry never stirred.

'Let me put it this way,' said Casson. 'You can hang as a gutter dog or as a jungle tiger. It is for you to choose, and it will be your last choice.'

Perry remained motionless, bowed over his knees. Casson was still also, still and quiet, but his heart was beating violently.

'How do I know you will do this?' asked Perry.

Casson opened the bound copy of the quarterly containing his article on the Witch of Bath. He laid it on the prison bed.

'Read that!' he said. 'I wrote it.'

Perry picked up the journal and began to read. He read very slowly and Casson could have screamed with the agony of impatience. Perry read three pages, turned to the end of the article and read the last paragraphs, shut the journal, and looked at its title page. He put it back on the bed.

'How do I know that you will do it?' he asked again. 'How do I know that it will be as you say? Duker,' he muttered. 'Duker!'

'If you observe your part of the bargain, I will observe mine.' Perry looked up sharply.

'There is a bargain, eh? I might have known it. It's a trap. I don't admit anything. You've been talking nonsense.'

'The bargain is this,' said Casson. 'If I write your story as I have said I will, you will tell it to me again, here and now, in your words and from the beginning. You will then plead guilty to the murder of Jim Macfarlane and you will write a confession of that murder. You need not mention the cases of blackmailing. They will be irrelevant; and if they do not appear in your trial they will be all the more startling when I produce them in my story.'

'You want a confession?'

'Yes.'

Perry laughed in jubilation.

'So you haven't got any evidence,' he said.

'In order to convict you,' Casson replied, 'we shall bring into Court every particle of the evidence which we have collected, especially about your blackmail. Lockyer will be a witness: so will Miss Martin: so will Mrs Gordonstoun: so will Jean Shaw. . . .'

'They'll refuse. They won't dare.'

'We shall subpoena them. Their evidence will build up to the murder of young Macfarlane – and to the one mistake you made. . . .'

'There was no mistake,' Perry interrupted. 'I'm sure there wasn't. I'm sure there wasn't.'

'Moreover,' Casson went on.

'What mistake?' Perry insisted.

'Moreover,' said Casson, paying no attention to him, 'I too will be a witness. The Court will not be interested in my analysis of your ambitions. It will not be interested in my interpretation of your career. It will take from me all the facts which I know: the facts only, nothing more, Those facts will be stale news when your trial is over. People will be bored with you. As a man you will be dead and as a story you will be dead. I want a confession of the murder: of that and of that only. The rest will be saved to surprise them in your biography.'

Perry took a turn up the length of the cell and back again.

'You will keep your side of the bargain?'

'I will.'

He took another turn up the length of the cell.

'How do I know it will be published? How can I be sure that people will read about me?'

Casson indicated the quarterly on the bed.

'That journal would print the story. But I would aim higher than that. A member of my Club wanted me to write for his newspaper. I shall offer your biography to him. He will take it.'

'You belong to a Club?' Perry asked quickly.

'I do.'

'Which one?'

'Cane's. Why?' What on earth was Perry driving at?

'Cane's,' Perry mused. 'Cane's. St James's Street. I should like to have gone into a Club before I died.' He looked at Casson with eagerness. 'Will you tell my story to the members of Cane's?'

'If you wish.' Casson wondered what the older members would make of it.

'They will talk about me,' Perry said, a strange look on his face which temporarily unnerved Casson. 'They will sit round the fire after supper and drink their dark, rich sherry' – Casson swallowed – 'and they will talk about me.' His voice altered in tone as he brought his gaze back to meet Casson's.

'But you will keep to your side of the bargain?'

'I will.'

'You promise me?'

Casson never hesitated.

'I promise.'

'Righty-o.' Perry leant back and breathed a long sigh of relaxation.

Casson rapped on the cell door and, when the constable put his head in, said:

'Bring me some paper. Foolscap. Lots of it. And a jug of water.'

'I want to make some notes,' Casson explained to Perry. 'Now, when you start telling me, start anywhere you like and just go on talking. I want to know everything. I'm your biographer. I'm Boswell to your Johnson.'

When the water came Perry drank half-a-pint of it right off and started talking. Casson was used to sitting up late but he became more and more exhausted, exhausted to the soul, as the insipid voice with its trace of accent talked on and on and on, detailing with relish its petty frustrations and the sly triumphs of its early life, its hates and jealousies: never its loves because it had none: except for statues and chairs and silver.

By the time Perry had finished the jug of water, it was ten minutes to four in the morning. The voice tailed off.

'Magnificent,' said Casson, coughing, his mouth raw from cigarette smoke. 'Now, one last thing: the confession.'

'Shall I write it?' Perry asked.

'Unless you wish to dictate it?'

'No. I'd like to write it myself.'

Casson pushed over some blank foolscap. Perry drew his chair up to the table and took his pen out of his breast pocket.

'You really ought to begin by saying who you are,' said Casson. 'You know. "I, John Henry Perry, of 51 Bickersteth Street, London w6 . . ." and then you go on. That's the efficient way.'

Perry started writing. He looked up.

'You only want the facts about the murder?'

'That's all. You'd better put in the motive.'

It took him fifty-five minutes to write it. He wrote slowly, pondering over words, sucking the end of his pen. He seemed to be writing with relish.

'There!' he announced as he put down his pen and handed the two sheets of foolscap to Casson. 'I think that will do. I think it is rather good. Shall I sign it?' Casson read it. It would certainly do. As a death warrant it was entirely adequate.

'Fine,' said Casson. He rose to his feet. 'Are you ready?'

'Ready?'

'To face the police.' Perry went stiff. 'And fame?' Casson added.

Perry drew in his breath and his mouth trembled. He looked sideways at the quarterly lying on the bed.

'Very well.'

Casson rapped on the door of the cell. He heard a yawn as the constable unlocked it again.

'Take us to the Superintendent,' he said. Perry followed them through the bleak hall of the station.

Casson went straight into the office, giving Perry no time to hesitate. Weldon was greyly unshaven in the sour yellow of the electric light. One of the Sergeants was asleep, and woke up with a jerk and a snort. Strutt's hair was rumpled and his tie and collar were undone. His fat face was puckered with strain.

Casson took the confession and laid it on the desk. Strutt seized it, glanced at Perry, and began to read. He finished it, looked at Casson, who was standing a pace behind Perry. Casson nodded. Strutt rose to his feet.

'I charge you, John Henry Perry, with the murder of James Robert Macfarlane. I caution you that anything you say will be taken down and may be used in evidence against you.'

No one moved.

'I plead guilty,' said Perry.

Strutt put the confession in front of him.

'Do you wish to sign this?'

'I do.'

'Read it through. To yourself. Not aloud.' Perry picked it up and read it through.

'It is true?' Strutt demanded as Perry laid it down again.

'Quite correct.'

'Then, if you wish, you may add: "I have read this statement, which I have made voluntarily, and it is true." Then, if you wish to do so, you may sign it.'

Perry fumbled in his breast pocket. He said in a faltering voice:

'I have left my pen in the . . . in the . . .' Casson thought that he was going to break down. It was a few seconds or failure. If Perry broke down now, he might panic and never sign.

Strutt gestured brusquely to one of the Sergeants, but the C.I.D.

man already had his own pen out and had placed it in Perry's hand. Casson was wearily amused to note that Strutt would not lend his own pen to Perry: whether it was from superstition or distaste he neither knew nor cared.

Perry signed. Strutt took out his own pen and witnessed. He straightened up again from the desk.

'Take him away,' he said.

When he had gone Strutt and Casson looked at each other.

'I'm going,' said Casson. 'I feel like doing penance.'

'Come and have a drink,' said Strutt.

The next Sunday Casson drove out to Putney. It was a morning of shimmering heat, gold pouring out of a sapphire sky. He stopped the Rolls in Disraeli Road.

Jean Shaw answered the bell.

'I thought you might care to lunch with me,' he said. 'We could go to Hurlingham.'

She hesitated for a moment.

'I'm sorry, Mr Duker,' she replied. 'I have another engagement.'

'I'm sorry too. Another time, perhaps.' She did not answer, but walked with him down the garden path. When they were at the gate she put her fingers on it to prevent it opening.

'You succeeded.' It was a blunt statement.

'Yes.'

'*You* did?'

'I did, Miss Shaw.'

She looked away.

'Will you tell me how?'

'I persuaded him to confess.'

'Persuaded? How?'

'I appealed to his vanity. I promised to write his story after he was dead.'

She looked at him.

'And you are going to do so?'

'No. He is a murderer. Worse than that. He has an unclean mind.'

'But you promised him?'

185

'I did.'

'Then – you must do it?'

'A promise not given on the heart, Miss Shaw, is not a promise.'

'Is it not – a matter of honour? I hated him but . . .'

'Honour among thieves?'

'Even among' – she hesitated – 'among all men?'

He opened the gate, and she made no motion to stop him.

'Good-bye, Miss Shaw.'

He climbed into his car and drove back to Mount Street. People are queer, he reflected. People are very queer.

John Perry was hanged at Brixton Prison at nine o'clock this morning. As I promised, I have written his story.

*Some more Penguin Crime
is described on the
following pages*

MURDER'S LITTLE SISTER

Pamela Branch

1947

'Did she fall or can we claim she was pushed?' That was the question.

Enid Marley shored up *You* magazine with a column for solving readers' problems. Her own were insoluble: her third husband had opted for a concubine and she wanted him back – badly, for appearances' sake. Suicide, she decided, might inject elastic into him – just a little suicide, not too much. But on the day she put her head in the oven, they were having a 'go-slow' at the gas-works.

Foiled in the home, Miss Marley made her big exit through the office window . . . and bounced on an awning five storeys below. (So foolish, you feel, when that happens.) Then it came back to her: someone had gripped her ankle up there. And that's not suicide, readers: that's going along to be murder.

In short, here's another dish of poisoned soufflé from Pamela Branch, as appetizing as *Lion in the Cellar* or *The Wooden Overcoat.*

'Anyone who can fail to laugh out loud here and there is a sad fellow' – *Guardian.*

Also available:
THE WOODEN OVERCOAT · 1354

DEATH UNDER SAIL

C. P. Snow

1953

The twin reputations of C. P. Snow, author of that massive sequence of novels which includes *The Masters* and *The Affair*, and Sir Charles Snow, the scientist whose name is associated with 'the two cultures', tempts one to wonder what kind of book such a man might have published in his twenties. *Death Under Sail*, his first novel, provides the answer. It is a tense and ingenious thriller.

The crew of *The Siren* were light-hearted at the prospect of three weeks' sailing on the Norfolk Broads. But when their host, Roger Mills, a Harley Street specialist, was found at the tiller of his yacht with a jovial smile on his face and a shot through his heart, all six guests – men and women – came under suspicion. And there, but for the detached and enigmatical Finbow, they might have remained.

'The complications are extremely ingenious; and the excitement is kept up to the end. . . . Even the most jaded detective-story reader will find a thrill and the most fastidious will find wit and feeling'
– *Observer*

NOT FOR SALE IN THE U.S.A.

BUMP IN THE NIGHT

Colin Watson

1966

Tuesday – fuse day. This is the association, fostered enthusiastically by the local press, beginning to take root in the increasingly apprehensive minds of the citizens of Chalmsbury. On three successive Tuesdays their habitual peace – some might call it torpor – has been shattered by explosions. Such landmarks as the drinking fountain and a statue of a late respected Colonel have been sent skyward; Chief Inspector Larch is baffled, and freely admits it. But after a Special Investigator has been called in, events take a more macabre turn. The fourth bang shatters not merely memorial stone and bronze, but human flesh and blood.

However, readers will be reassured to learn that the Investigator is none other than Inspector Purbright, familiar to many from Colin Watson's previous novel, *Coffin, Scarcely Used*. Once again he solves the problem, helped sometimes, but more often hindered, by a truly formidable collection of small-town characters.

'Genially obscene, pawkily funny, sharply observant, this is one of the most enjoyable crime stories I have read for months' – Julian Symons in the *Sunday Times*

'Lively characters and dialogue and a genuine mystery built in' – Maurice Richardson in the *Observer*

Ed McBain

'Ed McBain has terrific pace, an atmosphere of realism and smashing impact' – Erle Stanley Gardner

In a few short years Ed McBain has come crashing into the front rank of crime writers, both in print and on television. With toughness, reality, and genuine compassion he exhibits the cosmopolitan quarter of a big American city under the criminal end of the microscope. His cops of the 87th Precinct cling precariously to a life made lighter by some of the best wise-cracking humour in American fiction, and made safer by the most modern police techniques. This is 'kick-the-door-down' crime at its very best.

Ed McBain's first four crime stories are being published simultaneously in Penguins. They are:

COP HATER · 1968

Introducing Detective Steve Carella pitted against a ruthless cop killer.

THE MUGGER · 1969

Muggers snatch bags, and this one seems to be moving up into the murder bracket.

THE PUSHER · 1970

Carella wrestles with the ugly activities of the dope traffickers.

THE CON MAN · 1971

Teddy Carella, Steve's mute wife, runs a cold killer to earth.